short story Index

Winter's Tales 25

Winter's Tales
25

EDITED BY

Caroline Hobhouse

ST. MARTIN'S PRESS INC.
NEW YORK

First published in Great Britain by Macmillan London
Ltd 1979
First published in the United States of America in 1980

ISBN 0-312-88413-3

Library of Congress Cataloging in Publication Data

Winter's tales. 1—
   New York, St Martin's Press, 1955—
      v. illus. 21 cm. annual.

   1. Short stories
PZ1.W6792   808.83   55-13894

ISBN 0-312-88413-3

Contents

Acknowledgements

Martin Amis's 'Heavy Water' has appeared in *The New Statesman*, Murray Bail's *Healing* in the *New Yorker* and Elizabeth Troop's 'On Hearing the First Gigli in Spring' in *Fair Lady* (South Africa).
Peter Carey's 'He Found Her in Late Summer' appeared in *War Crimes* (University of Queensland Press, 1979)

Editor's Note

This twenty-fifth annual collection contains, I hope, the usual mix of stories by as yet little-known and well-known writers. I am especially glad to welcome three young Australian writers — Murray Bail, whose first novel *Homesickness* will be published by Macmillan next year, David Ireland and Peter Carey. None has previously appeared in *Winter's Tales*. Also new to the collection are Martin Amis and Clare Boylan.

Janice Elliott and Elizabeth Troop each have one previous appearance, and Gillian Tindall and John Wain (who first contributed to *Winter's Tales 2* in 1956) two.

Winter's Tales has now been in existence for longer than any other comparable British anthology and we have this year celebrated the fact in *Best for Winter*, a collection of twenty-five representative stories edited by A. D. Maclean. Meanwhile, we look forward to providing an outlet for the art of the short-story writer for at least another quarter-century.

C.D.H.

MARTIN AMIS

Heavy Water

JOHN AND MOTHER stood side by side on the stern
deck as the white ship back-pedalled out of the harbour.
Some people were still waving in friendly agitation from
the shore; but the great machines of the dock (impassive
guardians of the smaller, less experienced machines) had
already begun to turn away from the parting ship, their
arms folded in indifference and disdain. . . . John waved
back. Mother looked to starboard. The evening sun was
losing blood across the estuary, weakening, weakening;
directly below, the slivers of crimson light slipped helplessly over the oil-stained water, like mercurial rain off
fat lilies. John shivered. Mother smiled at her son.

'Tired and thirsty, are you, John?' she asked him (for
they had travelled all day). 'Tired and thirsty?'

John nodded grimly.

'Let's go down then. Let's go down. Come on.'

Things started heating up the next day.

'What, he's a bit mental, is he?' said Mr Brine with
hostile levity — 'A little bit mental?' Mrs Brine frowned
at her husband, as if in reproof; but really she was far
too drunk and happy to mind — as Mr Brine well knew.

'Yes,' said Mother simply, gazing across the deck to
the sea (where the waves were already rolling on to their
backs to bask in the sun). 'Yes, he is. Are you too hot,
John? Say if you are.'

'Does he always cry then?' said Mr Brine.

'Always,' consented Mother. 'It's his eyes. It's not that he's *sad*. The doctors say it's his poor eyes.'

'Poor chap,' said Mrs Brine. 'I do feel sorry for him.' Mrs Brine was in fact experiencing a hopeless pang of admiration and love for Mr Brine — Mr Brine, with his bronzed pot-belly, his holiday manner and his colossal cigar. 'What's his name? "John"? How are you, John? Enjoying your cruise, are you? Oh dear, look, he's crying again. Cheer up, John! Cheer up!'

The sea twanged in the heat. The sun came crackling across the water towards the big ship. John was six feet tall. He was forty-three.

John sweated helplessly in his charcoal-grey suit. He wore a plain white shirt — but, as always, an eye-catching tie. He showed no obvious signs of discomfort, and somehow his heavy, very mistaken clothing was one of the least incongruous things about him. It all suited John. He had a fat red face, the face of a scalded baby. His entire frame was fat, flowing, far more than anybody could need. His chin toppled into his chest and his chest toppled into his stomach; he had uneasy, protuberant, eunuchoid buttocks — and a little shy sprig for his manhood, which Mother would sometimes ruefully inspect. Water seeped and crept and tiptoed from his eyes all day and all night. It was his *eyes*. Mother loved him very much. There was nothing she would not do to cordon him off from pain.

'Yes,' said Mother, leaning forward reassuringly, 'he's still a child really — aren't you John?'

At seven o'clock every morning they were brought tea and the *Della Cruise News* in their cabin by the sighing young steward. John rolled heavily off the lower bunk and sat rubbing his eyes with his knuckles, very like a child, as Mother descended nimbly from above. She drank two cups of the boiling pink liquid, and then briskly fed John from his bottle — the same mixture as ever, the one she knew he liked. Next, grunting tenderly, she inserted his dripping dentures (as she withdrew her hand, silver threads of saliva would cling yearningly to her fingers — please don't take your hand away, please, not yet). She stood proudly by his side as he used the water-closet, inexpertly, sometimes abandoning his aim altogether, rearing back in awe of the mighty wash he had released. Mother mopped up. She clothed his cumbrous body, clicking her tongue with satisfaction as she furled the giant Windsor of his flaming tie.

'Do you want to go down for your breakfast now, John?' she asked in a light, rhetorical voice.

'Gur,' said John. ('Gur' was yes. No was 'Go'.)

'Come on then, John. Come on.'

In the submarine heat of the spacious, zigzagged dining-room, with its pearl-droplet lighting, Mother energetically consumed the full Grill — omelette, sausage, tomatoes, bacon and perhaps a kidney — while John enjoyed a soft-boiled egg, watched with predatory irony by Mr and Mrs Brine and by the other two guests at their table: a young man who had thoughts only for his sunbathing and the dazzling tan with which he intended to return to his ventilation-engineering plant in Croydon, and a beaky woman in her late thirties who came largely for the plentiful food and the lecherous officers (the food was indeed plentiful; the officers, on the other hand, usually turned out to be not quite lecherous enough). Soft, see-through white of egg would bobble hesitantly down John's face, pausing on his chin to look before it leapt on to the expanse of the serviette firmly secured to his chest by Mother.

At ten o'clock they attended the Singalong in the

Kingfisher Bar. And in this cramped and leathery venue they sangalong to the sounds of the Des Delano Trio. Or Mother did: John just wallowed with his head perched on his wide bent back, his liquid eyes bright, expectant. It was an apprehension of Mother's that John particularly relished these mid-morning sessions. Once, in the middle of a swirly Sinatra number which always took Mother back (the bus-shelter beneath the sodden Palais, larky Bill with his jacket on inside-out because of the rain, a single, teetering kiss), John jerked upright and let forth a deep guttural roar that almost put the band out of beat and earned a chuckling rebuke from handsome, dirty-minded Des when the song had been successfully completed. John grinned in furtive confusion. So did everyone else. Mother marched John back down to the cabin. She gave him a good talking to; and he never did it again.

Later they would take a turn on deck before repairing to the Cockatoo Rooms, where Prize Bingo was daily disputed. Again, John sat there stolidly as Mother fussed over her card — an abstracted, nest-proud sparrow, with new and important things to think about. He gave signs of animation only when the contestants wolf-whistled in response to the Caller's fruity 'Legs Eleven!' or when they chanted back a triumphant 'Sunset Strip!' to his enticing 'Sevenny *Sev*en. . . .' (The Caller was a queer, by the way, and made no secret of the fact, to Mother's disgust.) This morning she got eight numbers in a row and, surprising herself, yelped out *'House!'* as if exclaiming some shameful truth about her own life. John clapped his fat red hands — once, twice. Everyone near by smiled approvingly, except Mrs Brine, who watched Mother with blank and silent hatred. Mrs Brine didn't mind losing, but Mr Brine minded losing, and Mrs Brine minded that.

*

At about twelve-thirty John was given his mid-day bottle. Considerably refreshed, he would then diffidently squire Mother to the Robin's Nest for the convenient buffet lunch. (It took John a long time to get there: he always bumped into the corridor walls, like a man in a fast train, steadying himself slowly to the ship's roll.) With trays on their laps they watched through a hot glass window the men and women playing quoits and deck-tennis. Mother looked at John, slumped over his untouched food: he didn't seem to mind that he couldn't play. Mother smiled. Her Bill had been a fine sportsman in his day — bowls on the green, snooker, darts. . . . John was only — how old? — eighteen months when Bill went (the Civic Centre, scaffolding, calm insurance men finding fault). Well, what a year that had been! Barely a month after the funeral — with a feverish, nagging inevitability — little John's subnormality came to light; and for a long while Mother's life became the kind of tired riddle that wounding dreams set you to unlock. She buried Bill and, before the year was out, she'd had to put John back on the bottle, for good. Mother turned again. Now John slept, his chin tripled over his plump tie-knot, the four thin lines of water idly exploring his face, two from the corners of his mouth, two from his eyes, eyes that never quite went to sleep. Mother reached up with her serviette and wiped the tears away.

At five or so she gently massaged him awake. Waking was always a random and ticklish business for John; it was only with much painful endeavour that he could locate the bits of consciousness gingerly allotted to him. 'Better now?' she would ask. John nodded sadly. Then, together, hand in hand, they shuffled below to change.

For John, the evenings would elongate themselves in interminable loops and tangles — and he no longer tried to work them out. . . . Half an hour with Mother in the Parakeet Lounge, a friendly pinch on the cheek from Teri, tonight's Parakeet Girl (actually Teri lost her nerve at the last moment, and just skimmed her fingertips against John's face: she hadn't reckoned on the skin's slippery numbness. But never mind; no one noticed, not even John). Dinner in the Flamingo Restaurant — a fanned card-pack of evening wear. Mother went through the motions of encouraging John to eat something (she had his bottle ready but did not want to shame him in front of the Brines). John looked at the food: the food looked all wrong to John; to him, food never looked really dead. And he got into hopeless muddles and messes with his dentures (were they alive too?), and Mother stared. He ate nothing. On the way to coffee in the Robin's Nest, Mother liked to linger in one of the Fun Alleys. John stood behind her as she lost her nightly fiver on the stocky and powerful fruit-machines. She tugged and wrenched with her thin stiff right arm, like a machine herself in the jangling passageway. She never won anything. The other machines constantly and convulsively hawked out silver coins into their metal bibs (their keepers looking on coolly; even the nervous children won sometimes). But Mother's machine was giving nothing away, squat, smug, beaming, chockful of good things sneeringly denied to her. 'Maximise Your Pleasure By Playing All Five Lines,' said a sign above each machine, referring to the practice of putting in more than one coin at a time. Mother invariably tried to maximise her pleasure in this way, so she lost quickly, and they were never there for long.

What next? Time went slower as time went by. People wouldn't let the day go out of their hands: they wanted value, value. Every evening had its theme, and tonight was Talent Night — Peacock Ballroom, 10.30

sharp. Ranked couples eddied towards the double doors, the prismatic women with their handbags, the grimly spruced men with their drinks. They rippled in lines as the ship inhaled mightily, riding its luck. Someone flew out across the floor in a clattering sprint, hit the wall and fell over, heavily (a damson-jacketed waiter knelt down by the body, yelling out orders to a boy in blue). Mother steered John forward, through the doors, past the people candidly jostling for the better seats, and into the spangled shadows, where at length she wedged him between a back-row pillar and herself. 'All right?' she asked. John, hot, saturated, black-suited John, heaved up his head and looked dourly stageward as the lights went down.

There was a lady, nearly Mother's age, who performed a salacious, high-stepping Cockney number about prostitution, disease and penury — out of key and out of time, but with enough clockwork vigour to win the audience's contemptuous applause. There was a dear little boy — still at the Infants', they said — who completed a classical piece on the electric organ without once making a mistake. There was an elderly gentleman with a sturdy, well-trained voice who sang 'Bless This House' and, as a potent encore, 'If I Can Help Somebody.' Then a tall, sidling young man appeared and, after some confusion with the effeminate compère, unceremoniously proposed to drink a pint of beer without at any point using his hands: placing the tall brown glass on the floor, the man lowered himself mysteriously out of sight on the flat stage; a few seconds later his large, sandalled feet, quivering and very white, craned into view above the heads of the audience, the brimmed glass wobbling and slopping in their grip; there followed, in brisk succession, an abrupt crack and a harsh shout of anger and pain. ('Drunk,' thought Mother wearily as the man stood up, a hand clutched to his bleeding lips, and remonstrated with the scandalised compère). Mother got ready to leave. Who cared? There were never any winners. She poked John and directed a sharp finger at the end of the aisle. John made no response; he sat there, frowning, as the man on the stage gesticulated slackly at his hecklers. 'Sit *down*, woman,' said someone behind. Mother turned, glimpsing a clump of hate-knotted faces. She poked John again. 'Go,' he groaned. *Right then, my lad*, thought Mother, reaching down to give John's thigh a good pinch — the fleshy underside which was always so sore and chapped. John jolted, and with a weak snarl writhed upwards. No bottle for John that night, *oh* no. . . .

But John moaned with each intake of breath till well past midnight. Mother passed it down. Their hands touched. She had had it ready, anyway, just in case. She always did. She always would.

Now the ship was nearing Gibraltar and the pincers of the Mediterranean; and now the occasional foreign country would self-consciously present itself for view — over the littered and clamorous sun-decks where Mother dozed and where John sweated and stared and wept. Detailed announcements crackled over the Tannoy system. It hurt Mother's mind when she tried to make out what the man said; she just turned and gazed land-wards with a listless 'Look, John!' What was out there? Rippling green terraces salted with smart white villas. Distant docklands — once-thriving colonies where a few old limping insects still creaked about. A threadbare slope on which bandy pylons stood waiting. Then, too, the odd stretch of hallowed shore: the line of little islands like the humped coils of a sea-serpent, blank cliffs frowning angrily over the water at the ship, a pink plateau smothered in tousled grey clouds — all of it real and ancient enough, all of it parched, grand, indistinguishable.

In the course of its cruise the ship visited five key cities. During the first four stops John and Mother stayed on board. This was all right: many people did the same. As they approached the final port, however, Mother's anxieties steadied. She resolved to take John ashore. Why not? They were nearly home. Her mind was made up: she would take him ashore, for the experience.

But it was one of John's bad days. The impatient purser brought them tea an hour early, as agreed; and to begin with John simply refused to lift himself from his bunk. Calmly, wryly (this had of course happened before), Mother did what she always did when John was being difficult first thing; she filled his bottle, gave it a forceful shake — that violent drowning sound — and leant over his cot, where she swirled the liquid in inviting arcs above John's head. John prised open his thin scarlet eyes, and shut them again with a moan of — what? — fear? disgust? Mother blinked (this was new). Then with relief she recalled that she had given silly old John an extra half-bottle the night before, to curl up with, to help him sleep. Perhaps he had just lost his taste for it. But — 'Come on, my boy,' she said tightly, beginning to heave his soggy legs on to the cabin floor.

The touring-coaches, like a mirage of power and heat, wobbled at the quayside as Mother led John down the gangway and on to the scorched macadam. John stumbled. Mother clicked her tongue contentedly, realising that they would be the first on board. They sat side by side for thirty-five minutes as the coach filled up. The foreign cooling system made heavy weather of the heat. John shrank back from the canned air, already deafened by the bank of sun that glued him to his seat. Pools formed at all points of contact. Mother watched him, shrewdly supposing that now would be the time to re-submit the glistening bottle to his consideration. But she withheld it until the coach was toiling humidly down the coastal motorway. John held out his hand. He managed two swallows, three swallows. Screaming cars flashed past. John retched and dropped the bottle, his face melting. 'John,' said Mother. He stared at her through his tears for several seconds, then turned his drowned gaze on the boiling sea and its thousand eyes.

Mother hated the town. She hated the fat-trousered, incomprehensibly quacking guide, in whose rumpy wake they dawdled and idled like schoolchildren. Mother hated the lavatorial whiff, the leering touts, the tourists, the stringy lunch at the ramshackle hotel, where the Brines had crouched opposite John and laughed in whispers, making her think of all the pain she had had to deflect on his behalf. John sat tight, motion-less, silent, attempting nothing, dead to all his enemies.

After lunch the bowing guide was dismissed (after a round of bitter applause) and the ship's officer told them with the aid of a megaphone that they had an hour to shop and souvenir-hunt before reassembling in the square. Hesitantly Mother led John down an alley, about a hundred yards from the coach bay, and came to a determined halt. She was going no farther: something might happen. For a few minutes she dejectedly admired the flamboyant curiosities in the window of a tourist shop. Then she turned and looked up — and at once her spirits climbed. There at the corner of the alley stood a large sign (plain as day, in English) welcoming visitors to the Municipal Aquarium. She urged John forward with some eagerness. John had never been in an aquarium before. . . .

The building was small, dark, low-ceilinged and fume-laden; and, apart from a kind of baby's swimming-pool in the centre of the room (in which an apathetic turtle grimly wallowed), there were just a dozen or so square tanks built into the walls, shimmering like televisions. Well, what else can I do with him? thought Mother as, with no real prospect of pleasure, she tugged John towards the first tank and proceeded to shuffle round. Gradually, however, she became pleasantly absorbed and entranced by the unexpected echoes of colour and tone. There were some frilly sea-anemone things (all the stickered tags, of course, were in a language she'd hardly heard of) that looked just like Mrs Brine's smart turquoise bathing-cap, with its spiky locks. Coin-shaped mooners bore the same leopard-dots and zebra-flashes as were to be found among the dramatic patterns of the ship's Parakeet Lounge. Flounced, refracted, absurdly dressy fish weaved among the dunce's-hat shells and cracked coral. Three whiskered, toothless old-timers took a constitutional on the turgid surface as, well beneath them, in the tank's middle-air, a lone silvery youngster flickered about, as if nervously testing its freedom. From the adjacent stalls the lobsters, cripples with a dozen crutches, watched the random activity with malevolence and despair, reaching up boney fingers as if to pluck at their own stark eyes. Teddyboy snakes on the sandy floor, straightening their skin-tight trousers, fish in funny hats with bottomless beads for eyes, crabs like the apoplectic drunks in the Kingfisher Bar. . . . Mother was enjoying herself vastly by the time she guided John to the final tank. They stopped; they gazed. There was nothing but an arched hollow of freckled stone, and still water. Mother was about to sigh and move towards the door when a completely non-descript grey fish — a sardine, a sprat — burst from the brown hollow. It stared out. It flew around, seeking the extent of its confines. It paused, darted, paused, as if embarrassed by its own trapped dumb ordinariness. It stared; it stared from the depths of its marinated eternity. With a sobbing gasp John wheeled away from her into the alley and the air, and with violent jolts of his hunched shoulders barked out great cataracts of reds and whites that Mother couldn't for the life of her remember him eating.

The next day, back on board the ship, just before dinner, John got lost for a little while.

John was sitting on his bunk as Mother rinsed his bottle in the bathroom. The connecting door swayed shut in the gentle swell. Shaking the flooded bottle (going, going), Mother opened the door and stepped into the cabin. John wasn't there.

'Oh my darling, what have you done?' said Mother.

Negotiating steep swerves of panic, Mother lurched out into the corridor. A passing white-shorted officer looked at her with concern. She turned away guiltily. Where would he *go*? In a migraine haze her eyes groped through the Parakeet Lounge, the Cockatoo Rooms, the Kingfisher Bar. . . . No John. Where would he *go*? Up, up.

John faced the evening alone at the very stern of the ship, a hundred feet above the writhing furrows of its wake. Spreading his arms, he received the bloody javelin hurled at him by the sun. Then, his heavy limbs working slowly, he tried to scale the four parallel white bars that separated him from the sea. Over and over again, as in a drunken dream, he placed his right foot on the first rung, both hands firmly gripping the fourth, and each time he lifted his left foot from the deck he toppled backwards in a heap, and gathered himself up, and placed his right foot on the first rung. . . .

Why? What was the sea hissing in his ears? What raw sun tugged at his eyes? His hands grew red and slippery in the salted wind, but still he tried, the right foot, the hands, the left foot, the fall. Mother watched. Mother watched him try — two times, three times. She moved calmly down the steps from the sun-deck to the broad stern. She knew that she had won then.

'Go,' sobbed John. 'Go, *go*.'

She walked him down to the cabin. He came quietly. She sat him on the bunk. She started to sing a soothing lullaby. John wept into his hands. There was nothing new in Mother's eyes as she reached for his bottle, and for the gin, and for the clean water.

MURRAY BAIL

Healing

THE QUALITY of miracles has declined over the years In Adelaide, a flat city, 'the city of churches', we all went around on bikes. I am speaking here of the mid-nineteen-fifties. My father, for example, rode an Elliott. It was a heavy machine, bottle green, with leather cleaning bands rolling around the hubs, silver-frosted handlebars, and a seat sprung with two thick coils like hair curlers. My father with his grey face and his pitted bike clips: arriving home after the Magill Road climb, he'd lean the bike under the grapevine and rest in the darkened kitchen with a sarsaparilla. It was a three-mile ride from where he worked. Yet — and I still believe this — our bikes and the pedalling past dry hedges somehow signify the period, the white light and optimism of the fifties. They fit in very well. The man across the street subscribed to *The Saturday Evening Post*. Things just seem more complicated now.

I said Adelaide is a flat city. Well, it is and it isn't. It looks flat on the map or from the air, but the wide intersecting streets contain an inbuilt slope of private dimensions, barely perceptible, often invisible to the naked eye. The city centre is located halfway between the sea and the perpetual purple backdrop, the Adelaide Hills. Our days consisted of coasting into the hot empty air, then pushing slowly back towards the hills. Magill Road here was a classic. It ran from the foot-hills to

town, about four or five miles, straight and smooth,
wide and harmless-looking. But try cycling up one day.

It was on Magill Road, about a third of the way
down, that I saw the accident. I was one of the few.

Denis Hedley was considered a smart alec. His bike
was an Elliott, like my father's, but he had stripped it of
the mudguards and painted the frame canary yellow and
black. Around the wheel rims he'd painted a chequered
flag pattern, which at low speed made old people dizzy.
But its most conspicuous feature, and the thing that
attracted ridicule, was a plastic aeroscreen he'd fitted, as
on a racing motorbike, over the handlebars. The handlebars were black and horizontal, also like a motorbike's.
Hedley had made them from a piece of pipe. Closer
inspection — though we tried not to give Hedley the
satisfaction — revealed other significant modifications.
Every possible strut and clamp, even the bell, the wing
nuts, and parts of the pipe frame had been drilled with
holes to save weight. Hedley was too smart to talk
much, but he confided casually one day it gave him
extra speed. And it was a blurred yellow-and-black fact
that he dominated the upper reaches of Magill Road.
Crouched behind the aeroscreen, legs pumping like
wheels, Hedley would streak past trams and the small
British sedans at thirty-five or even forty-five miles an
hour and, reaching the Burnside Road intersection,
which is near our street, would suddenly sit up and
coast no-hands, sometimes combing his hair or scratching the small of his back. Then he'd brake, turn around,
and laboriously climb back for another run. That was
how afternoons were spent in Adelaide. He was thick-
necked and of course had pimples and oily hair. He
wore tight khaki shorts. Hedley was also well known for
his fourteen-year-old sister, Glenys. She had damp hands
and a cowlike smile. She was the first girl in our district

to suddenly begin wearing a brassière.

On this particular morning, my chain had come off and I was squatting down by the footpath. It was a quiet Sunday, hot; not many cars. As I say, I was one of the few to see everything. I happened to look up as Hedley went past. He had Glenys sitting sideways on the top bar — something I had not seen before. I could see they were going too fast. Hedley seemed to be struggling with the handlebars; Glenys was rigid, holding too hard. As they passed No. 1839 Magill Road — which oddly enough, I realise now, was the year the bicycle was invented — Hedley's specially lightened frame appeared to buckle slightly, or fold, and because of his indiscriminate drilling this placed sudden strain on the brake-drum strut. It snapped. It had been drilled too much. The back wheel then slid forward, throwing the chain and all hope of braking. What followed could only be called a chain reaction. The atrophied pipes of Hedley's bike, the drilled and countersunk sprockets and levers, all began cracking and splitting, the little aeroscreen flew into the air, bits of broken metal and spokes fell off and jumped all over empty Magill Road like black sparks. The machine, no longer a bicycle, began weaving and contracting, approaching the intersection.

And then from behind came Boardman (that rings a bell!) on his mauve Healing. It was the latest model, with alloy guards, three-speed gears; Boardman was the local Healing dealer. As usual, he was riding with a lighted cigarette. With superb balance and strength for a thin man in his forties, with tremendous cool, he rode in close and, pedalling in top, lifted Glenys off and on to his serene handlebars. By then Hedley's tangle was almost at ground level, still sparking at high speed, and Hedley had one leg trailing. Again, Boardman leaned over and down, this time more like a polo player, and grabbed Hedley by the collar, supporting the careering machine and halting further disintegration, while with the other hand he applied the chrome-plated brake calipers on the Healing, weaving to a halt across the intersection. At the last second Hedley lost his grip. His bike somersaulted in the clarity of that Sunday morning, snapped around the veranda post of Townsend's corner shop, and lay in two or three pieces. Glenys's blouse was badly torn; I could see her ochre brassière. She immediately began swearing at her brother, and I realised she had grown up. She was no longer a girl.

Hedley stood there, one shoe missing, surveying the wreck. Boardman lit up another cigarette, waved, and rode off. I have not seen anything like it since. Boardman is dead now, and I don't know if they make Elliotts anymore. Hedley and his sister must still be alive, grown up. My father is dead. A Shell service station has replaced Townsend's corner shop, and the intersection has been fitted with lights.

CLARE BOYLAN

Appearances

THE WIDOW gave my mother a pair of boots. They were biscuit-coloured with little pointy toes darkened with polish. The heels were shaped like an apple core and gave the feet a rising curve that made me think of the neck of a pony. 'They're kid boots,' my mother said, shocked. The widow nodded. She had clutched them to her breast like infants. She handed them across. They were set in the centre of the table and the two women watched them with sadness. 'You're too good,' my mother said, confused. 'They're too good.' 'Just so they get some use,' the widow said. Her eyes found me under the table and she gave me a long look like Christ crucified, so forgiving that I had to suck my lips in over my teeth. She stood up painfully and skushed away in her black sandals.

'She was very beautiful,' my mother said. The boots still held the centre of the table, a monument to her beauty. We had arranged the tea things around them. 'Like a young Indian girl, ebony hair braided in plaits, skin the colour of honey.'

She met her husband at the post box. They were posting letters to other people who were forgotten in that instant. Ten years later, when she was thirty, he stepped in front of a motor car and turned her into a widow. She buried her beauty with him She took a lodger in the upstairs room and sold paraffin from a shed at the end of the garden leading to the lane.

A frond of rhubarb jam dangled through a hole in my toast. I sucked it through from underneath. I had heard the story before. Each time the widow brought us an instalment of her past, Mother repeated it as though it was her task to tend the memories. All I had to do was listen but I did so with a face bulging with disbelief. The widow was not beautiful. Her skin was grey. She was stooped and seamed with sadness. All women were sad but some had the toughened crusts of good old times built into them. It gave them a sense of privilege. The widow's sadness was a mildew that overgrew and enclosed her.

Her young husband took her to France on a boat. They saw the Eiffel Tower and drank wine at tables in the street. He bought her new boots, kid. Nothing was too good for her.

'Put them on. Put them on. Let's see!' Mother chuckled as if she had suggested something wicked. We were both caught up in glee. I tore off my own boots with the laces still tied and flung them anywhere. The soles flapped and gaped like corner boys' and they sailed across the floor. 'They're sieves! You poor daisy!' Mother lamented. We doubled up with laughter.

I was eleven, nearly twelve. My legs were no longer rigid stalks of sinew. When I stretched them out one by one to pull on the boots my mother peered and frowned on their new curve and sheen. They had become miraculously fleshed and golden as a cake does in the oven. I pulled on and she did the buttons. It took a long time and made us serious again. I was a big child. My feet almost filled out the dainty toes. 'Now walk,' she said. I levered myself down from the chair and took a few blunted steps — a hoofed animal. I began to giggle. Mother sighed. 'It's a shame, but they'll have to do.'

I tottered over to her and stopped. 'I'll take them off now.' She did not look at me. 'No. Keep them on. You've got to get used to them.'

She started to clear the table, clattering the dishes as if I had done something to annoy her. She would not look at me. 'Your boots are in tatters,' she accused. 'You have me disgraced among the neighbours.'

Disgrace was a shameful word. To be poor was the greatest disgrace of all. My father had left us when I was four although Mother always said he was working abroad. He sent us a little money now and then. Spread very thinly, it was made to do. Close to the top of our meagre shopping list came Appearances. Mother kept a tablet of Pears' soap in a tin in the hot press. I could always tell when visitors were coming because I was sent to the press to bring the soap to the bathroom. I can still remember the exact feel and smell, its tortoise-shell transparency, coming out of a nest of cellophane in a butterscotch tin. Sometimes it was thin and had to be pried off with expertise like a new scab. In the end it became a golden monocle which I was allowed to take to my bath, viewing through a sepia haze the coal fire in front of which the metal tub was placed, before going to bed smelling of visitors' hands.

On the kitchen press, beside the china dog with glass eyes, the soap jar was kept. It was where mother saved up coins for a fresh tablet, knowing it was one of the few things that mattered; knowing, like everyone else, that poor people used cake soap.

She was strong and good. She was also stubborn. There were times, as now, when nothing one might say would make sense. Children had appearances to keep up too. It was not the sort of thing one could explain to an adult. Insignificance was our aspiration. Conformity was all, the trappings of womanhood taboo. High heels were pantomime farce. They belonged to another world that did not incorporate walking, skipping, running, scuffing, climbing. Those delicate leather points had nothing to do with my own square and practical feet. It was hopeless to imagine that I could prance into school like a centaur and not be made to suffer. I would not wear them, never. I would bring my own boots in a bag and change in the park, hide the kid boots in a bush. I caught my mother's patient glance. She was sitting at the table again, very still, hands folded like flower petals. Her hands were not like flower petals but the evening sun was suddenly a flurry of pink tissue paper which lit up the frizzy gold of her hair and her pale, unhappy mouth, rose-tipped her fingers.

She smiled on my scowling rage with such pure affection and amusement that for a moment she looked lovely and I worshipped her. For a moment. I smiled, regretted it, became confused and clumped out of the room and off to bed like a pig on a pogo stick.

School was two miles from where I lived and I was given twopence each day for the tram. In the morning I walked to school and saved a penny for an Eccles cake for the Owl. Walking was no hardship. Most of the girls walked. We did not stride out with unhappy stoicism as people do today snorting up the air as if it was a ball of string to be sucked up the nostrils in a single, tortuous breath for the good of their health. We stalked and ambled like cats, sniffing at the air without particularly taking it in, scenting incident on the wind. Girls collected girls as they streeled along. There was no organised pattern but it was not aimless. Navy-blue arms intertwined. Heads bowed, profiles blurred. The girls stamped along.

'Got anything to eat?'

'Me lunch. Lay off.'

'Cheese?'

'Jam.'

'Keep them.'

'Spell "miscellaneous".'

'M-i-s-s. . . .'

'That's the easy one. Gilhawley'll kill you.'

'She can't kill me.'

'No.'

'She can't kill me. She can't kill me. She can't kill me.'

'What have you got on your cheeks?'

'Nothing. What's the stuff on your eyes?'

'Nothing.'

'Are they there yet?'

'I don't know. I won't look.'

'Neither will I.'

'They're there.'

'Fools.'

'Ignoramuses.'

Two unhappy schoolboys now trotted behind. On no account would they be permitted to walk beside us for we had heard that one could become pregnant that way. We spoke to them only in insults. They did not speak to us at all. Each group of girls had a similar colony of misery bringing up the rear. They were our boy-friends.

In spite of frequent threats to our lives from the homicidal Miss Gilhawley and other unpredictable adults, I can scarcely ever remember waking with anything other than happy anticipation. There were exceptions. The morning I opened my eyes to the hateful glittering toes of the boots was one. It took me twenty minutes to do the buttons. My fingers shook with ire. I limped downstairs and understood that there was no hope of walking to school. I would have to face the Owl without an offering.

On the tram I felt deformed with misery. The Owl had not spoken to me, had not pulled my hair. When I boarded the bus he had given my legs a shocked look, glanced at my face in angry query, but I would not look at him. I slid into a seat and stared out of the window. Several times I could feel his gaze on my stupid boots and on my face as if he felt I owed him an explanation. There was nothing to say. I could not let my mother down by making him understand that we were poor. He would have to believe that I had grown mad and indifferent.

When I stepped from the platform in geriatric fashion at my stop he was still watching me that way. I wanted to race away and hide my shame. I could only mince like a Chinese lady, feeling the critical tawny eyes on my back as the tram clanged off down the street. There was a dead cat flung inside the school gates and I kicked its jammy-looking corpse with one polished toe from Paris.

The Owl was my name for our tram conductor. He was a little dark man in early middle age with strange orangey eyes and a long nose and a small, cheery mouth. In spite of liberal oiling, his black hair sprang into hundreds of small curls that resembled clusters of blackcurrants. His real name was Herbert. He did not know my name. He called me his pigeon, his herring, his little hen. The names caused a queer nervous chill in the pit of my stomach, a contradictory boiling flush on my face. I wanted to be crushed in his arms — and more — a nameless something, not imagined, deeply known. He was my Owl. Oh, how I loved him. My mind raced about miserably while my eye slumped on a page of a history book which impersonally mated myth and fact and celebrated the deaths of millions.

'Napoleonic Wars! You, miss! You with the boots! Dates?' I had a white shirt, a wine tie and a navy gymslip. I had navy stockings and navy knickers, but boots were what Miss Gilhawley specified.

Boots were what identified me from thirty-four other girls in the class. My feet hurt, my heart hurt. I lifted hurt eyes to the teacher but she saw only the non-absorbent eyes of an idler. 'Vain and idle woman,' she hissed. 'You are the bane of my life.' I hid in the toilets during lunch, ate my brawn and biscuits in the smelly dark. When school ended I fled as fast as my crippled heels allowed praying that I might be on the tram and on my unhappy journey home before the girls came. At the gate I tripped on the cat's corpse and landed with that peculiar flying sprawl so familiar in childhood. Blood and gravel flourished on my knees and palms. A clump of girls circled over my scattered body. They were not my friends but an opposing group, big and evil. 'She's wearing women's boots! She's wearing women's boots. Find her a husband! Put them to bed! Give her a baby!' they chanted. My two best friends hung back. They were embarrassed by my appearance and afraid of the tough girls. I glared up at their big, unkind faces, their lumpy bosoms under gymslips, their ugly knees. My hands scrabbled for some object of retaliation — and clutched. I got on my feet. I swung out in a wide arc with the dead cat, holding on to its tail, exhilarated at my perfect aim as the little fanged, matted jaw clouted each girl's face into expressions of dumb horror.

'They're *not* women's boots,' I panted. 'They're *kid* boots!'

The lingering pleasure of victory prepared me to withstand the Owl's indifference on the tram. He had looked at me with some curiosity when I clambered on board, muddy and bloodied in my high heels. He had glanced expectantly at my right hand to see if it guarded the baker's bag which carried his customary afternoon treat. There was no bag, no Eccles cake. He turned away and went down the aisle jingling change in his fist. I limped to a seat and concentrated on cleaning the worst of the gore from my skin with a hankie.

'Here, let me help.' A low voice close to my ear. The tram was almost empty and the Owl had settled himself on the edge of the seat opposite. He licked a rather crumpled handkerchief and began to dab at my knees. He did it with tenderness. I could only stare. His face looked different. Normally his eyes crinkled at the corners. They were wide open now, peering over my dirty knees and troublesome boots as though he had mislaid something and expected to find it concealed amidst the blood and endless buttons. 'I do like your boots,' he said softly. 'Very dainty they are.' He put his handkerchief in his pocket and scrubbed his hands together, workmanlike. 'Bloody kids,' he grumbled. 'They grow up that fast.'

When some people got on the tram he stood up very straight and moved away so briskly that I was left to wonder if I had imagined his look. He had liked my boots, though, very dainty. No one had ever called me dainty. My elongated toes pointed the way to a breath-taking world of enchantments and vanities. If I could have danced I would have danced.

Later, when I was swinging on the platform as we drew near to my stop the Owl materialised once more. 'What age are you?' he breathed against my hair. 'Thirteen.' 'Good child,' he said. 'Quite the young lady, very lovely.' He asked me if I ever took the air in the park. 'I go every Saturday,' I said rapidly. Having already lied about my age I saw no advantage in confessing that I passed most afternoons in the cinema, spending the money I earned on Saturday morning, lighting fires and stoves for the Jews. The boys sat in a row behind us and passed sweets to us over our shoulders.

'I could meet you there, at the pond,' he murmured. 'There's something I want to show you.' I nodded. The hammering of my heart made me feel sick. 'Good child,' he said.

The pavement was still moving towards me when I jumped. I had to do a little skitter like a music-hall turn to keep my balance.

Mother noticed my cut hands and knees. She made a rueful little mouth of sympathy. 'Had a good day?' she said. I nodded. I still could not speak. She looked as if she might say more but instead she came to me and pressed my head against her breast, stroking my hair fiercely. 'Good child,' she said.

I was going to have a baby. The thought made me feel important. I would have to take the belt off my school tunic and bring a pint of milk to the classroom for my lunch. If the girls pasted me I would have a miscarriage. There would be buckets of blood on the school steps. I sat in the pokey grass at the edge of the pond and scraped sugar grains from the top of an Eccles cake with my teeth. In a bag tucked into the lap of my yellow frock was another cake. That was for the Owl. The cakes had been paid for by the Jews. I got twopence for lighting their fire and putting a match to the jets on the gas cooker. Mrs Wolfson and her two daughters, Gilda and Tilly, had forsworn housework on Saturdays. The girls locked their plump fingers under their breasts and sang duets, easing their brown eyes and dimpled faces into mists of love while they smiled at their father, who was very small.

Mrs Wolfson accompanied on the piano. She kept a glass of wine on top of the instrument for her refreshment. She wore a long silk dress the colour of wine and a garland of black feathers round her neck. Her dress was cut low at the front to show breasts which rose evenly like successful loaves. The drawing-room was a treasure trove. Each piece of furniture was veiled with lace like a bride. There were glass lamps and silk cushions and little crystal dishes of sweets. After my work I was allowed to choose a sweet from one of the dishes. I had to sit in a marshy velvet sofa to eat it. Gilda sank down beside me, embracing me in ladylike smells. 'Now, who is the lucky fellow?' she said straight away. I grimaced coyly and squirmed with rage. 'There is no fellow,' I said. 'So!' she clasped her hands and surveyed me efficiently. 'You have waved your hair for no fellow. You have put pink on your cheeks and grease on your lips for no fellow. You have borrowed someone's high-heeled boots for no fellow.' The other members of the family watched me with smiling interest. 'He is not a fellow,' I said coldly. 'He's a grown man. He wants to show me something.' The women glanced at one another darkly. Their chins drew back and their breasts billowed forward until they looked like some very peculiar birds.

'How would your mother feel if you told her some grown-up man wanted to show you his something?' Mrs Wolfson said angrily. 'I bet he's got a wife,' said Gilda. 'I bet his wife has seen enough of his something.' 'You stay away from this man,' Tilly said. 'As sure as black is white you will have a baby.'

He had a wife. I had seen them one Sunday afternoon on the beach at Killiney with about half a dozen little currant-haired children who screamed in ragged delight

at the waves. The children all had dirty faces. Even
when they ran into the water and the waves broke over
their heads they emerged with streaks of dirt glistening
under the wet. Mrs Owl was fat. She wore a pink
bathing-cap and swimming costume although she stayed
on the shingle. She lay back on a rug chewing sand-
wiches and cuddling a dirty baby. He chased the
children into the water and ran back to his wife,
proclaiming his pleasure with a grin. For a reply she
threw back her head and chortled. I watched his squat
brown figure, like a modern cartoon of a peanut man,
shepherding his family with mirth. His hair bubbled and
gleamed like boiling oil. His amber eyes crinkled. My
stomach cringed.

In the park the afternoon heat summoned up its
swarm around the pond. Young women pumped the
handles of prams to maintain the trussed human
contents below explosion point. Courting couples
crouched tensely entwined. Elderly gentlemen stepped
out briskly with walking-sticks and followed feebly with
inefficient feet. Two boys of nine or ten blundered by
in sullen grey jackets and dusty boots. Their appearance
caused such a sensation of outrage among the calm
possessors of the pond that they galloped off like
spiders into the dank trees. If the adults saw me at all
they saw a nice quiet child in a yellow dress. If I saw
them, I saw them as aspects of my scenery, of no more
individual significance than cows or ducks. Grown-ups
were parents and teachers and people behind shop
counters. I did not think of them as part of my future
any more than I thought of death. To me it was a children's world. Adults were people who were too old to be
children. Deprived of all that they knew and that made
them happy, they grew mad and dangerous. They ate
unpleasant food and emanated pungent smells. They

were angry and violent and constantly had to be forgiven. Men and women locked themselves behind doors together and moaned and argued with restrained madness. They did curious things together of which children were warned but not told. The Owl was a grown man. This fact had impressed the Wolfsons greatly. Tilly had declared that I would have a baby.

In my mind's eye I could see her glistening carmine lips compressed in envy, her breasts swollen like a bolster in awe; now, in my real eye, my Owl approaching, striding past the ornamental pagoda and the flower borders, coming to show me something adult and undoubtedly curious. I felt important and, curiously — grown-up.

I finished a last moist and delicious mouthful of fruit and flaky pastry and licked crumbs and sugar from my lips. I brushed the skirt of my frock and spread it over my legs like a fan. A few people looked when I waved with both arms to the Owl. My Owl. He looked wonderful. He was specially dressed up in a pale cotton jacket and a blue shirt open at the throat. He plodded towards me with his head down as if it was an uphill climb. I jumped to my feet and extended my hands to him. He scowled into the grass and hurried past, in the direction of the trees where the boys had vanished. I swung my unwanted arms and stared after him, mouth gaping with hurt. After a few moments I swooped to pick up my paper bag and raced after him.

He was guarded by a circle of elms. He had taken off his jacket and it swung stylishly from a branch. He smiled at me now, his crinkly smile.

'That's right, chicken,' he said when I approached.

'You ran away,' I whined.

'Not from you, pigeon. There. I've got something to show you, something special. It's a secret. We don't want the world and his wife looking on.'

'I've brought you a cake.'

'That's my girl.'

I came to him holding out the bag in both my hands. He did not take the bag but put his hands around my wrists and very slowly brought his mouth down to my forehead. It landed like a scrap of paper. He led me away, still holding my wrists in his hands. We wandered through dim, luminous, wooded paths. We came to a rather unpleasant part of the park where there was a dried river-bed and a writhing tangle of tomato weeds. Ill-tempered walls of briar guarded the pit which had once been a piece of a river. It was a place famed for unpleasantness. Children were warned not to go there. He picked me up in his arms. My long legs spilled over his limbs. He surged recklessly through the thorns, clutching my skirt in a bunch to keep it from tearing. He put me down on a mossy patch that was olive green and velvety. He sat opposite to me. Our feet touched on the ground.

'You've always been special to me,' he said.

'I love you,' I said.

'Oh, well,' he said.

'I'd do anything in the world for you. I'd die for you.'

'Hush now. Let me talk.' He reached out a hand to touch my face, but did not. His fingers traced my body without touching it. He dropped his hand to my leg and clutched the oddly curved ankle of my boot. 'You've always been different from the other kids — noisy little buggers. I feel you understand me. There's not many people understand. I'd have spoken before but I thought of you as just a little girl. Forgive me, miss. . . . It wasn't until you ventured into ladies' boots that I saw you as a lovely young woman. I'm a married man, of course, and you're still only a young lass, but every dog's entitled to his day.'

I had begun to be afraid. I was not used to being treated as an equal with adults. It was certain to mean trouble. My mouth was dry. My limbs went prickly. I looked up at the high walls of briar, the relentlessly blue sky, praying that someone would pass or rain descend.

'Do you trust me, miss?' he said. I nodded. 'What I'm going to show you is something very sacred, something private. You must promise not to tell a living soul.' I nodded. 'Good child.'

He began to unbutton his shirt. I stared in awful curiosity. 'Don't look yet, pettie,' he urged. 'Close your eyes and don't look until I say.' I clenched my eyes. 'Look at me now! Look at me now!' his voice commanded. I opened my eyes and slammed them shut again. I had been struck blind. Where the Owl had sat nothing remained but a blaze of light. I looked again, cautiously. The Owl was still there, a frowning blur of face in the shadows. He was dressed in a cotton vest and trousers. The entire surface of his vest was pinned with silver medals. Caught in the low rays of the afternoon sun they flashed and glimmered like unnatural fire. I clapped my hands in delight and gazed in wonder on my beautiful Owl, my wizard.

He moved closer. He caught my hand and pressed it to his metallic chest. It made a musical jangle. He said: 'You can touch them if you like.'

I began to explore the dazzling engraved miniatures. The Owl's chest was populated by a lot of unhappy-looking men and women in long dresses. Rays of light came out around them and there were messages written in Latin. 'That one's been blessed by the Holy Father in Rome,' the Owl narrated. 'This is a miraculous medal of the Blessed Virgin. Wear it at all times and it keeps you safe from harm. See the little glass door on this. It's a sacred relic of a saint. It carries a plenary indul-

gence to save you from hell in case of mortal sin. This is
Saint Christopher, patron saint of travellers. That heart
is the Sacred Heart of Jesus, burning with love for you
and me. Here's Saint Jude, patron saint of hopeless
cases.' Together we explored each member of his powerful and passionate family and thrilled at their magical
powers. I thought I had never seen anything so wonderful in my life. The Owl said he had been a sodality man
all his life. He had other medals and relics at home,
hundreds. He could accommodate no more under his
clothes. He had to keep them under his clothes because
there were those who would snigger at holy things. His
wife even smiled a bit sometimes. I was different. He
had known from the start that I would understand.

I understood. I burned with understanding. I felt that
the Owl and I stood alone in all the world, enclosed in a
radiant shape like the Sacred Heart.

There were things I still did not understand and after
we had sat in silent understanding for some minutes I
began to wonder about them Had I now been taken
across the terrible threshold of womanhood? It did not
matter, of course, nothing mattered. It would just be
sensible to know. I put my hands around his bristly
neck and kissed him quickly to show that I did not mind.
'Are you giving me a baby?' I asked. His orange eyes lit
on me in astonishment. He seized my hands and pulled
them roughly away. 'Bloody kids,' he complained.
'You haven't been listening to a blessed word I said.'
He tore the paper bag which was lying at my side. He
took out his cake and began to chew on it, angrily and
rather hungrily.

PETER CAREY

He Found Her in Late Summer

HE FOUND HER in late summer when the river ran
two inches deep across glistening gravel beds and lay
resting in black pools in which big old trout lay quietly
in the cool water away from the heat of the sun.
Occasionally a young rainbow might break the surface
in the middle of the day, but the old fish did no such
thing, either being too well fed and sleepy or, as the
fisherman would believe, too old and wise to venture
out at such a time.

Silky oaks grew along the banks and blackberries,
dense and tangled, their fruit long gone into Dermott's
pies, claimed by birds or simply rotted into the soil,
vigorously reclaimed the well-trodden path which
wound beside fallen logs, large rocks, and through
fecund gullies where tree ferns sent out tender new
fronds as soft and vulnerable as the underbellies of
exotic moths.

In one such gully a fallen tree had revealed a cave
inside a rocky bank. It was by no means an ideal cave. A
spring ran continually along its floor. Great fistfuls of
red clay fell frequently and in the heat of the day
mosquitoes sheltered there in their swarming thousands.

Three stalks of bracken outside its dirty mouth had
been broken and the sign of this intrusion made him
lower his hessian bag of hissing crayfish and quietly
peer inside.

It was there he found her, wild and mud-caked, her hair tangled, her fair skin scratched and festered and spotted with infected insect bites. She was no more than twenty years old.

For a long time they regarded each other quietly. He squatted on his heels and slapped at the mosquitoes that settled on his long, wiry brown legs. She, her eyes swollen, fed them without complaint.

He rolled down the sleeves of his plaid shirt and adjusted his worn grey hat. He pulled up his odd grey socks and shifted his weight.

She tugged at her dress.

At last he held out his hand in the way that one holds out a hand to a shy child, a gentle invitation that may be accepted or rejected.

Only when the hand was lowered did she hold hers out. It was small and white, a city hand with the last vestiges of red nail-polish still in evidence. He took the hand and pulled her gently to her feet, but before a moment had passed she had collapsed limply on to the muddy floor.

Dermott adjusted his hat.

'I'm going to have to pick you up,' he said. It was, in a way, a question, and he waited for a moment before doing as he'd said. Then, in one grunting movement, he put her on his shoulders. He picked up the bag of crayfish and set off down the river, wading carefully, choosing this way home to save his passenger from the blackberry thorns which guarded the path along the banks.

Neither spoke to the other, but occasionally the girl clenched his shoulder tightly when they came to a rapid or when a snake, sleeping lightly on a hot rock, slipped silkily into the water as they approached.

Dermott carried his burden with pleasure yet he did

not dwell on the reason for her presence in the cave or attempt to invent theories for her being so many hundred miles from a town. For all of these things would be dealt with later and to speculate on them would have seemed to him a waste of time.

As he waded the river and skirted the shallow edges of the pools he enjoyed his familiarity with it, and remembered the time twenty years ago when it was as strange to him as it must be to his silent guest. Then, with the Old Inspector, he had done his apprenticeship as his mother had wished him to, read books, learned to identify two hundred different dragon-flies, studied the life-cycle of the trout, and most particularly the habits of the old black crayfish which were to be his alone to collect. It was an intensive education for such a simple job, and he often reflected in later years that it may not have been, in an official sense, compulsory, but rather a private whim of the Old Inspector who had loved this river with a fierce protectiveness.

The examination had been a casual affair, a day trek in late spring from where the old Chinese diggings lay in soft mossy neglect to the big falls five miles up-river, yet at the end of it he had successfully identified some two hundred trees, thirty insects, three snakes, and described to the Old Inspector's satisfaction the ancient history of the rocks in the high cliffs that towered above them.

It was only much later, after a child had died, a wife had left and floods had carried away most of his past, that he realised exactly what the old man had given him: riches more precious than he could ever have dreamed of. He had been taught to know the river with the quiet, confident joy of a lover who knows every inch of his beloved's skin, every hair, every look, whether it denotes the extremes of rage and passion or the quieter, more subtle, moods that lie between.

Which is not to suggest that he was never lonely or that the isolation did not oppress him at times, but that there were few days in which he did not extract some joy from life, whether the joys be as light as the clear web of a dragon-fly or as turbulent as the sun on the fast water below Three Day Falls.

The winters were the hardest times, for the river was brown and swollen then and crayfish were not to be had. Then he occupied himself with a little tin-mining and with building in stone. His house, as the years progressed, developed a unique and eccentric character, its grey walls jutting out from the hillside, dropping down, spiralling up. And if few walls were quite vertical, few steps exactly level, it caused him no concern. Winter after winter he added more rooms, not from any need for extra space, but simply because he enjoyed doing it. Had ten visitors descended on him there would have been a room for each one, but there were few visitors and the rooms gave shelter to spiders and the occasional snake which feasted on mice before departing.

Once a gipsy had stayed during a period of illness and repaid his host with a moth-eaten rug of Asiatic origin. Other items of furniture were also gifts. An armchair with its stuffing hanging out had been left by a dour fisheries inspector who had carried it eighty miles on top of his Land Rover, knowing no other way to express his affection for this man on the river with his long silences and simple ways.

Books also were in evidence, and they were an odd assortment. Amongst them was a book on the nature of vampires, the complete works of Dickens, a manual for a motor-car that now lay rusting in a ravine, and a science fiction novel entitled *Venus in a Half-shell*. He had not, as yet, read any of them although he occasionally picked one up and looked at it, thinking that one day he would feast on the knowledge contained within. It would never have occurred to him that the contents of these books might reflect different levels of truth or reality.

'Nearly home,' he said. They had left the river and passed through the high bracken of Stockman's Flat. He trudged in squelching boots along the rutted jeep track that led to the house. He was hot now and tired. 'Soon be there,' he said, and in a moment he had carried her through the thick walls of his house and gently lowered her down into the old armchair.

She huddled into the armchair while he filled a big saucepan with water and opened the draught on the stained yellow wood stove.

'Now,' he said, 'we'll fix you up.'

From the armchair the girl heard the words and was not frightened.

There was about him a sense of pain long past, a slight limp of the emotions. His grey eyes had the bitter-sweet quality of a man who has grasped sorrow and carries it with him, neither indignant of its weight nor ignorant of its value. So if his long body was hard and sinewy, if his hair was cut brutally short, there was also a ministering gentleness that the girl saw easily and understood.

He brought warm water in a big bowl to her chair and with it two towels that might once, long ago, have been white.

'Now,' he said, 'one of us is going to wash you.'

He had large drooping eyelids and a shy smile. He shifted awkwardly from one water-logged boot to the other. When she didn't move he put the towels on the arm of the chair and the bowl of water on the flagstone floor. 'Don't worry about getting water on the floor,' he said.

She heard him quelch out of the room and, in a moment, imagined she heard a floor being swept elsewhere in the house. Outside the odd collection of windows she could see the tops of trees and below, somewhere, she heard the sound of the river.

She picked up a grey towel and went to sleep.

The tin roof was supported by the trunks of young trees. The stone walls were painted white, veiled here and there by the webs of spiders and dotted with the bodies of dead flies. In one corner was a bed made from rough logs, its lumpy mattress supported by three thicknesses of hessian. A tree brushed its flowers against the window and left its red petals, as fine and delicate as spider legs, caught in the webs that adorned the glass.

She lay naked on the bed and let him wash her.

Only when he came in embarrassed indecision to the vulva did she gently push his hand away.

When the washing was over he took a pair of tweezers, strangely precise and surgical, and removed what thorns and splinters he found in her fair skin. He bathed her cuts in very hot water, clearing away the yellow centres of red infections, and dressed each one with a black ointment from a small white jar which bore the legend 'For Man or Beast'.

He denied himself any pleasure he might have felt in touching her naked body, for that would have seemed wrong to him. When the wounds were all dressed he gave her an old-fashioned collarless shirt to wear for a nightdress and tucked her into bed. Only then did he allow himself the indulgence of thinking her pretty, seeing behind the cuts and swellings, the puffed eyelids, the tangled fair hair, a woman he might well have wished to invent.

She went to sleep almost immediately, her forehead marked with a frown.

He tiptoed noisily from the room and busied himself tidying up the kitchen in a haphazard fashion. But even while he worried over such problems as where to put a blackened saucepan his face broke continually into a grin. 'Well,' he said, 'wonders will never cease.'

When dinner came he presented her with two rainbow trout and a bowl of potatoes.

It would be two days before she decided to talk and he passed these much as he would normally have, collecting the crayfish both morning and afternoon, gardening before lunch, fishing before dinner. Yet now he carried with him a new treasure, a warm white egg which he stored in some quiet, dry part of his mind, and as he worked his way down the rows of tomato plants, removing the small green grubs with his fingers, he smiled more often than he would have done otherwise.

When a shadow passed over the tangled garden and he looked up to admire the soft drift of a small white cloud in the very deep blue sky he did not look less long than he would have normally but there was another thing which danced around his joy, an aura of a brighter, different colour.

Yet he was, through force of habit, frugal with his emotions, and he did not dwell on the arrival of the girl. In fact the new entry into his life often slipped his mind completely or was squeezed out by his concentration on the job at hand. But then, without warning, it would pop up again and then he would smile. 'Fancy that,' he'd say. Or: 'Well, I never.'

The girl seemed to prefer staying in the house, sometimes reading, often sleeping with one of Dermott's neglected books clutched to her chest. The swellings were subsiding, revealing a rather dreamy face with a wide, sad mouth and slightly sleepy blue eyes. A haze of melancholy surrounded her. When she walked it was with the quiet distraction of a sleep-walker. When she, sat, her slow eyes followed Dermott's progress as he moved to and fro across the room, carrying hot water from the fire to the grimy porcelain sink, washing a couple of dishes, or one knife or two forks, stewing peaches from the tree in the garden, brewing a herb tea with a slightly bitter flavour, sweeping the big flagstone floor while he spread dirt from his hob-nailed boots behind him, cleaning four bright-eyed trout, feeding the tame magpie that wandered in and out through the sunlit patch in the back door.

He whistled a lot. They were old-fashioned optimistic songs, written before she was born.

When, finally, she spoke, it was to talk about the sweeping.

'You're bringing more dirt in than you're sweeping out.'

He did not look surprised that she had spoken but he noted the softness of her voice and hoarded it away with delight. He considered the floor, scratching his bristly head and rubbing his hand over his newly shaven chin. 'You're quite correct.' he said. He sat on the long wooden bench beneath the windows and began to take off his boots, intending to continue the job in stockinged feet.

'Here,' she said, 'give it to me.'

He gave her the broom. A woman's touch, he smiled, never having heard of women's liberation.

That night at dinner she told him her story, leaning intently over the table and talking very softly.

It was beyond his experience, involving drugs, men who had abused her, manipulated her, and finally wished to kill her. He was too overwhelmed by it to really absorb it. He sat at the table absently cleaning a dirty fork with the tablecloth. 'Fancy that,' he would say. Or: 'You're better off now.' And again: 'You're better off without them, that's all.'

From the frequency of these comments she judged that he wished her to be quiet, but really they were produced by his feeling of inadequacy in the face of such a strange story. He was like a peasant faced with a foreigner who speaks with a strange accent, too overcome to recognise the language as his own.

What he did absorb was that Anna had been treated badly by the world and was, in some way, wounded because of it.

'You'll get better here,' he said. 'You've come to the right place.'

He smiled at her, a little shyly, she thought. For a brief instant she felt as safe and comfortable as she had ever been in her life and then fear and suspicion, her old friends, claimed her once more. Her skin prickled and the wind in the trees outside sounded forlorn and lonely.

She sat beside the kerosene lamp surrounded by shadows. That the light shone through her curling fair hair, that Dermott was almost unbearably happy, she was completely unaware.

Weeks passed and the first chill of autumn lay along the river. Dermott slowly realised that Anna's recovery would not be as fast as he had imagined, for her lips remained sad and the sleepy eyes remained lustreless and defeated.

He brought things for her to marvel at: a stone, a dried-out frog, a beetle with a jewel-like shell, but she did not welcome the interruptions and did not try to hide her lack of interest, so he stood there with the jewel in his hand feeling rather stupid.

He tried to interest her in the river, to give to her the pleasure of the Old Inspector had given him, but she stood timidly on the bank wearing a dress she had made from an old sheet, staring anxiously at the ground around her small flat feet.

He stood in the water wearing only baggy khaki shorts and a battered pair of tennis shoes. She thought he looked like an old war photo.

'Nothing's going to bite you,' he said. 'You can stand in the water.'

'No.' She shook her head.

'I'll teach you how to catch crays.'

'No.'

'That's a silky oak.'

She didn't even look where he pointed. 'You go. I'll stay here.'

He looked up at the sky with his hands on his hips. 'If I go now I'll be away for two hours.'

'You go,' she insisted. The sheet dress made her look as sad as a little girl at bedtime.

'You'll be lonely. I'll be thinking that you're lonely,' he explained, 'so it won't be no fun. Won't you be lonely?'

She didn't say no. She said, 'You go.'

And he went, finally, taking that unsaid no with him, aware that his absence was causing her pain. He was distracted and cast badly. When a swarm of caddis-flies hatched over a still dark pool he did not stay to cast there but pushed on home with the catch he had — two small rainbows: he had killed them without speaking to them.

He found her trying to split firewood, frowning and

breathing hard.

'You're holding the axe wrong,' he said, not unkindly.

'Well, how should I hold it then?'

She stood back with her hands on her hips. He showed her how to do it, trying to ignore the anger that buzzed around her.

'That's what I was doing,' she said.

He retired to tend the garden and she thought he was angry with her for intruding into his territory. She did not know that his mother had been what they called 'a woman stockman' who was famous for her toughness and self-reliance. When she saw him watching her she thought it was with disapproval. He was keeping an anxious eye on her, worried that she was about to chop a toe off.

'Come with me.'

'No, you go.'

That is how it went, how it continued to go. A little litany.

'Come, I'll teach you.'

'I'm happy here.'

'When I get back you'll be unhappy.'

Over and over, a pebble being washed to and fro in a rocky hole.

'I can't enjoy myself when you're unhappy.'

'I'm fine.'

And so on, until when he finally waded off down-stream he carried her unhappiness with him and a foggy film came between him and the river.

The pattern of his days altered and he in no way regretted the change. Like water taking the easiest course down a hillside, he moved towards those things which seemed most likely to minimise her pain. He helped her on projects which she deemed to be important, the most pressing of which seemed to be the long grass which grew around the back of the house. They denuded the wild vegetable garden of its dominant weed. He had never cared before and had let it grow beside the tomatoes, between the broad leaves of the pumpkin, and left it where it would shade the late lettuce.

As he worked beside her it did not occur to him that he was, in fact, less happy than he had been, that his worry about her happiness had become the dominant factor of his life, clouding his days and nagging at him in the night like a sore tooth. Yet even if it had occurred to him, the way she extended her hand to him one evening and brought him silently to his bed with a soft smile on her lips would have seemed to him a joy more complex and delightful than any of those he had so easily abandoned.

He worked now solely to bring her happiness. And if he spent many days in shared melancholy with her there were also rewards of no small magnitude: a smile, like a silver spirit breaking the water, the warmth of her warm white body beside him each morning.

He gave himself totally to her restoration and in so doing became enslaved by her. Had he been less of an optimist he would have abandoned the project as hopeless.

And the treatment was difficult, for she was naked and vulnerable, not only to him, to the world, but to all manner of diseases which arrived, each in its turn, to lay her low. In moments of new-found bitterness he reflected that these diseases were invited in and made welcome, evidence of the world's cruelty to her, but these thoughts, alien to his nature and shocking for even being thought, were banished and put away where he could not see them.

She lay on his bed, pale with fever. He picked lad's love, thyme, garlic and comfrey and ministered to her with anxious concern.

'There,' he said, 'that should make you better.'

'Do you love me, Dermott?' she asked, holding his dry, dusty hand in her damp one. They made a little mud between them.

He was surprised to hear the word. It had not been in his mind, and he had to think for a while about love and the different things he understood by it.

'Yes,' he said at last, 'I do.'

He felt then that he could carry her wounded soul from one end of the earth to the other. He was bursting with love.

As he spent more and more time dwelling on her unhappiness he came to convince himself that he was the source of much of her pain. It was by far the most optimistic explanation, for he could do nothing to alter her past even if he had been able to understand it. So he came to develop a self-critical cast of mind, finding fault with himself for being stubborn, silent, set in his ways, preferring to do a thing the way he always had rather than the way she wished.

Eager to provide her with companionship, he spent less and less time on the river, collecting the crays just once, early in the morning while she slept. In this way he lost many but this no longer seemed so important.

When she picked up a book to read in the afternoons he did likewise, hoping to learn things that he might share with her. He felt himself unlettered and ignorant. When he read he followed the lines of words with his broken-nailed finger and sometimes he caught her watching his lips moving and he felt ashamed. He discovered things to wonder at in every line and he often put his book down to consider the things he had found out. He would have liked to ask Anna many things about what he read but he imagined that she found his questions naïve and irritating and did not like to be interrupted. So he passed over words he did not understand and marvelled in confused isolation at the mysteries he found within each page.

The True Nature of Vampires had been written long ago by a certain A. A. Dickson, a man having no great distinction in the world of the occult whose only real claim to public attention had been involved with extracting twenty thousand pounds from lonely old women. Needless to say, none of this was mentioned in the book.

Dermott, sitting uncomfortably on a hard wooden bench, looked like a farmer at a stock sale. He learned that vampirism does not necessarily involve the sucking of blood from the victim (although this often is the case) but rather the withdrawal of vital energy, leaving the victim listless, without drive, prey to grey periods of intense boredom.

On page ten he read:

The case of Thomas Deason, a farmer in New Hampshire, provides a classic example. In the spring of 1882 he befriended a young woman who claimed to have been beaten and abandoned by her husband. Deason, known to be of an amiable disposition, took the woman into his home as a housekeeper. Soon the groom and farm workers noticed a change in Deason: he became listless and they remarked on the 'grey pallor of his skin'. The groom, who was a student of such matters, immediately suspected vampirism and, using rituals similar to those described in the Dion Fortune episode, drove the woman from the house. It was, however, too late to save Deason who had already become a vampire himself. He was apprehended in a tavern in 1883 and brought to trial. After his conviction and execution there was still trouble in the area and it was only after a stake was driven through the heart of his exhumed corpse in 1884 that things returned to normal in the area.

One night, when making love, Anna bit him passionately on the neck. He leapt from her with a cry and stood shivering beside the bed in the darkness.

Suspicion and fear entered him like worms, and a slow anger began to spread through him like a poison, nurtured and encouraged each day by further doses of A. A. Dickson's musty book. His mind was filled with stories involving marble slabs, bodies that did not decompose, pistol wounds and dark figures fleeing across moonlit lawns.

He eyes took on a haunted quality and he was forever starting and jumping when she entered the room. As he moved deeper and deeper into the book his acknowledgement of his own unhappiness became unreserved. He felt that he had been tricked. He saw that Anna had taken from him his joy in the river, turned the tasks he had enjoyed into chores to be endured.

He began to withdraw from her, spending more and more time by himself on the river, his mind turning in circles, unable to think what to do. He moved into another bed and no longer slept with her. She did not ask him why. This was certain proof to him that she already knew.

Yet his listlessness, his boredom, his terrible lethargy did not decrease, but rather intensified.

When the jeep arrived to pick up the crayfish its driver was staggered to see the haunted look in

Dermott's eyes, and when he went back to town he told his superiors that there was some funny business with a woman down at Enoch's Point. The superiors, not having seen the look in Dermott's eyes, smiled and clucked their tongues and said to each other: 'That Dermott, the sly old bugger.'

He had nightmares and cried in his sleep. He dreamed he had made a silver stake and driven it through her heart. He dreamed that she cried and begged him not to, that he wept too, but that he did it anyway, driven by steel wings of fear. He shrieked aloud in his sleep and caused the subject of his dreams to lie in silent terror in her bed staring into the blackness with wide-open eyes.

He thought of running away, of leaving the river and finding a new life somewhere else, and this is almost certainly what he would have done had he not, returning from a brooding afternoon beside the river, discovered the following note:

Dear Dermott, I am leaving because you do not like me anymore and I know that I am making you unhappy. I love you. Thank you for looking after me when I was sick. I hate to see you unhappy and I know it is me that is doing it.

It was signed: 'With all the love in my heart, Anna.'
The words cut through him like a knife, slicing away the grey webs he had spun around himself. In that moment he recognised only the truth of what she wrote and he knew he had been duped, not by her, but by a book.

It was evening when he found her, sitting on the bank of a small creek some three miles up the jeep track. He said nothing, but held out his hand. They walked back to the river in darkness.

He did not doubt that she was a vampire, but he had seen something that A. A. Dickson with his marble tombs and wooden stakes had never seen: that a vampire feels pain, loneliness and love. If vampires fed on other people, he reflected, that was the nature of life, that one creature drew nourishment and strength from another.

When he took her to his bed and embraced her soft white body he was without fear, a strong animal with a heavy udder.

JANICE ELLIOTT

Going Home

HE WOKE to find her shaking his arm. He felt that his chest was crushed beneath a hoop of iron. He lay still waiting for it to shift.

'You were shouting. Was it the dream again?' Her face was a pale disc above him. He pushed himself up then swung his legs out from under the sheets so that he was sitting on the edge of the bed, his back to her. Breathing was better now, the sweat dried coldly on him. She sank back but did not close her eyes. 'You should see someone. It's not just the dreams. Aren't you getting in again?'

'Not worth it.' He walked round the end of the bed to the door and put out his hand but he only touched her shoulder. 'Go back to sleep.'

In the small room where Sally had slept when she was a baby — they had not been in this house when Michael was born — he put on the same suit he had worn to work yesterday. After he had gone to bed his wife had hung it up and put out a clean shirt and a clean pair of socks. Opening the louvered cupboard doors to find a tie, he snuffed a closeted, powdery sharpness, hers.

There was a remarkable clarity, everything more than usually defined. He flicked a switch on the control-board by the oven and a light came on at the base of the coffee percolator. The refrigerator hummed into its cycle. The table was laid for breakfast. When the cornflakes were finished, but not before, Michael would be allowed to cut out the month's offer and send 30p for the Mr Spock ray-gun. Sally still used her baby bowl. He read: 'Bobby Bear went to the Moon one day, Fishing for Starfish I've heard say.' No message there. Pot of hyacinths on the dresser, too pink, blindingly sweet. School terms dates, notice about P.T.A. meeting pinned up on red felt-covered board with Mick's latest masterpiece: two massive tanks on collision course, jet fighters, big-bellied bombers laying bombs like eggs, very small stick-insect people, black. Papers on mat: bombs, Ireland, floods, famine, drought, Rod Stewart marriage on/off/on.

The garden was full of sun, tarpaulin still over the sand-pit but bulbs pushing through already. The corner of the lawn was in shadow. He saw himself cross the bright grass and sit on a deck-chair in the shed. His wife did not go there. Spades clotted with earth, paperback Orwell surviving its second winter here and the attentions of mice. *I should not like to be shot for having an intelligent face, but I do agree that in almost any revolt the leaders would tend to be people who could pronounce their aitches.* Can't drop my aitches now, used to, sometimes if I'm drunk, my party turn. The shed smelled of his father, who had never seen it. There was a bit of wood Michael had been trying out his new penknife on, shaping something. He picked it up, tried to follow the wavering intentions of his son's imagination, and put it in his pocket. His heart broke.

She would think he'd gone off early.

He saw her with the children in the kitchen, lit from here like a stage. She was softer in the morning, blurred, she wandered around the kitchen in her housecoat giving the children breakfast, drinking coffee, lit a cigarette, squinted into the sun. Michael went alone to the primary round the corner, Sally would be picked up and carried off to nursery school.

The children left. She sat down, lit another cigarette, poured more coffee, then she got up and scraped the plates into the bin, picked up the papers, sat down. A small neat woman, dark, who could never quite make up her mind if her womb hampered or fulfilled her — her only bewilderment, a touching one. She looked at the *Guardian*, frowned, wondering what was the matter with her husband.

He slipped out through the little gate at the end of the garden and got into his car. Driving through the suburbs, he was dazzled as he had been on waking by the crashing brilliance of minutiae: a child's anorak throbbed red, a man standing on a pedestrian overpass, like a country stroller watching a river, was haloed in light. At a traffic block in Mill Hill a long black Mercedes drew up alongside him. He saw a child with eyes like toffee, two veiled women wearing white gloves, and a wolfhound. At the same moment they all turned and looked at him.

At any time he might have changed his mind and taken his bursting heart back to the woman in the kitchen. *I cannot breathe in this electric house in this city, this marriage, though I love you most dearly: the years lie on my breast like sand.* He could have said. Since time had struck him dumb he had conducted many such unspeakable monologues in his mind addressed to wife, children, father, friends, strangers, the living and the dead. Now the M.1 peeled away before him, a straight line north, home. Home? He settled back in his seat, flicked the radio to Vivaldi and felt the iron hoops ease. He breathed better, was aware of hunger.

He saw himself. His spirit cruised comfortably above him like an angel, observed how cleverly he parked the car, pushed open the glass doors, walked to the counter, took a tray and, accompanied by his angel, set out on the table eggs, bacon, sausages, tomatoes, tea, thick white bread and butter. Children's high-tea food. Nancy and I do not eat breakfast in the electric house. Up cholesterol. The artery walls thicken leading to sluggish circulation and heart failure. Ah, the heart is a tender, treacherous organ, a brave little pump bearing one up mountains, through a number of energetic beds (the act of love equivalent to a five-mile walk), but so terribly subject to breaking. And aching. My father's burst as he walked down the summer garden path to cut a cabbage. He was a small, neat, faithful man, with dry hands.

Some old men die in bed with young mistresses. Infidelity strains the heart.

So does time, obesity, smoking, anger and responsibility.

'Aren't you going to eat that?'

She looked like all the young do nowadays: hair that might have been gold tormented into a wild frizz, half Afro, half Burne-Jones; a paisley smock thing, the kind of garment worn long ago by good children bowling hoops in picture books; duffle bag; grubby purple crochet shawl; twang of Cockney in her accent — classless, the way they all talk now. Good strong face though, clear gaze.

'Because if you aren't, could I have it?'

Preposterous. Bloody cheek. But then, why not? He pushed the plate towards her, went on smoking. She ate fast but thoroughly, with the fastidious energy of a cat. No thanks, but equally, no offence. A clean transaction, no strings. He took pains not to be watching her (why?), lit another cigarette, looked at the electric clock over the Formica bar. A man who gives away breakfasts must have somewhere to go.

'Will you give me a lift?'

'You don't know where I'm going.'

'Doesn't matter.'

He shrugged.

'Which is your car?'

'That one.'

'Nice.'

She walked out ahead of him to the car. Her feet were bare, but quite clean. She settled in the seat, experimented, lowered it till she was nearly lying flat, stretched her legs out straight, closed her eyes. His angel, who had condoned his flight, so helpfully escorted him thus far to a sensible breakfast, pardoned even his anorexia, saw this latest rashness as a motorway pick-up, unworthy of the high adventure. Sourly, he folded his wings.

She awoke without shock, as the young can, as he imagined she always did. She had a very faint golden down, he noticed, all over her skin.

'Why do you smoke so much?' There was a freshness about her, she asked questions because she genuinely wanted answers, just as she had wanted the breakfast. *Free* came into his mind, and *brave*.

'Habit, I suppose. Filthy habit.' Programmed, defensive responses. We've all got to go. At least I don't rape little girls or beat my wife. Ho ho ho. Nan so forbearing. No one smoked nowadays. Darling, find Daddy's ciggies.

'Do you like it?'

'I hate it.'

'Then throw it away.'

'No.' Bugger you, child, with your open face.

She liked that. Surprise. For the first time she smiled. She flicked on the radio with her toe and Beethoven came belting out. *Tarara-boom-di-ay . . .I'm sitting on a tomb-di-ay*. Sweet, sad Chekhov, fifteen years ago with Nan at the Lyric, Hammersmith. He found that he was laughing. The bright road peeled away. They set behind them wedges of England, began to enter his country.

'Bradbury. Alan Bradbury.'

'Mandy.'

'Amanda?'

'Miranda.'

They ate pies as they went along. He did not want to go into houses. She had a bottle of water in her duffle bag.

'Good. You've cheered up. You had a long face back there.' She asked questions but made no demands. He could have stopped the car, reached across to open the door and told her to get out. He had a comfortable feeling of himself in the car, a riding soul in a chariot on a road on the planet in space. He wanted to tell her this.

Bradbury named the town to which they were going. 'I'm an architect. There might be a site.'

A slight impatient nod. She knew this was not the whole story. As they put the miles behind them he felt Nan and the children grow smaller until they seemed to be waving from a little raft.

The motorway ran through a deep cutting. He turned off into a feed-road which started broad then narrowed and climbed, setting them on an eminence above a valley. The trees were still black here and sparse, there was a snap of snow in the air. Bradbury was a heavy man: his thick corded neck acknowledged the weight of his head; in the south he lumbered, displacing too much territory; here, in the open, on the hard ground, his gravidity was right.

The girl sat to the left of him and a little behind on a dry-stone wall, with the car rug draped round her shoulders. Her face was pinched with cold, almost ugly, the strong planes sharpened. He turned back and smiled choosing to be anxious for her.

'You'll get starved.'

She slipped off the wall and came up behind him. She rested one hand lightly on his shoulder, with the other held the rug around her. Across the valley a black town was piled on the hill. There was no colour at all in the landscape but Bradbury was eased as if he were sitting before his own hearth.

The girl said: 'I've never been this far before.'

He couldn't believe it.

'Oh, all over, of course, North Africa, Spain. I lived in Spain — that was all right.' She explained: 'But I've never been up here. It's different, isn't it? You look different when you're looking at it. You come from here, don't you?'

He nodded.

Back in the car, Bradbury felt a sudden spit of temper towards the girl, because she had seen how he felt. He wanted to be angry with her.

'Why don't you wear shoes? You ought to wear shoes.'

'Why?'

'Because your feet will get cold.'

She smiled, fiddled with the radio and began to hum. They drove on. She curled up on the bench seat, her offending feet tucked under her. She turned up the radio. Something raw and rackety. Bradbury snapped it off, drove stiff-faced.

The girl was laughing at him.

'You shouldn't do this,' he said. 'Hitch lifts from men.'

'Are you going to rape me?' Not coy or even remotely provocative, just straight out, wanting to know. 'I wouldn't mind if you did.'

'Then it wouldn't be rape, would it?'

'I could put up a fight?'

'Not today, thanks.'

'What's she like?'

'Who?'

'Your wife.'

At this point the mill-stream ran by the road, on the other side the river: fast cold water over stone. His father walked by the river on a summer evening — look, boy, a dragon-fly. At this point, as you entered the valley, it was like going through a passage, between walls of granite. Bradbury pulled in just before the bridge. He felt nothing.

He leaned across and opened the car door. 'Get out,' he said.

It was dark when he got into town. The one good inn had changed — all flash and Formica — but they could put him up. Why should it not have changed? Why should they know him? He had thought of the past contained, in pockets of time.

In his room he flopped out on the bed, smoking, then picked up the telephone. Nan's voice: 'Hello? Hello. Alan, is that you?' Television in the background, the children shouting, his warm, sweet home. Nan would have a hand over one ear, the receiver to the other. 'Where are you, Alan?'

Bradbury replaced the receiver and immediately the telephone rang.

'Nan?'

Reception said his friend was waiting in the bar.

No mistaking that starved, bird-boned nape, crowned by the electric frizz.

'Oh, good. I was getting thirsty.'

'What the hell are you doing here?'

She grinned. 'Worked it out. Only one place you'd be, wasn't there? I'll have a pineapple juice.' She was getting some looks in the bar but not as many as he expected — times had changed up here too. 'And I wouldn't mind a pie.'

He put down the glasses and the plate. 'You'll spoil your supper.'

'I like food.'

'So I've noticed.' Bradbury drank. After the pie she had a sausage. 'I'm sorry. I shouldn't have chucked you out like that.' There was something so sure about her, a rootlessness he envied. Living in the south he had been a tree torn out. Not entirely people — not people at all. A certain topography he'd been bred in, he told himself. (Lift up thine eyes to the hills? Hardly. He'd spent half his life getting away and the other half wanting to be back, with hardly an interval between; or so it seemed.)

And now he was here? Nothing.

But for some reason he wished to owe her something.

'I suppose I wanted to be alone. But I'd no right to take it out on you.'

'Could I have another sausage?'

He flung back his head and laughed. He felt in some way redeemed.

The restaurant had gone up in the world, anyway. Spanish waiters, French menu, carafe wine from God-knows-where and candles in bottles. Bradbury loved to watch her eat but she wouldn't touch the wine.

'Why not?'

'Life's a high, isn't it?' She sucked her chicken bone.

Later, over Irish coffee in the residents' bar, 'Where are you going to sleep?'

In the end, he got her a room but at some time in the night she slipped into his, and when Bradbury woke at dawn she was snoring on the floor in the skinny sleeping-bag she kept in her duffle. He'd been dreaming of Nan.

'D'you want to come in here?'

Miranda made love exactly as she ate, with hunger and impersonal pleasure. She didn't kiss much. The smallest breasts he'd ever seen. She knew what she wanted, too. No, she said: like that, here, please? Grinning, her small teeth showing: 'D'you like that?'

'You sound like a bloody waitress.'

'Shut up, lie back and enjoy it.'

'Help, help,' he cried, 'this is rape!'

When they'd finished — or he'd finished with her or she with him — she just curled up and fell into a deep sleep he guessed to be dreamless. By now the city was beginning to form outside the window: the houses and the chimneys and the spires, the factories and guarding hills took shape.

She came up behind him. 'Snow!' she said, and he smiled.

'I thought I hated the stuff. But not this morning. We'll have to get something to put on your feet, though.'

There was a shoe-shop round the corner. He took her measurement and brought back long red boots with ridiculous heels, adding on impulse a short rabbit coat. She accepted them with glee but without thanks, as she took anything given to her — as she herself would have given, if she had anything to give. She stalked around the room, naked but for the jacket and the boots. 'Kinky,' she said. 'Filthy old man.'

*

They had given up any pretence of looking for a site. They drove to the edge of the moors and here the snow had not melted but lay in streamers between the dark crags. From here you could see seven counties.

'When I was a lad I thought this was where the devil brought Christ.' But he guessed the past meant nothing to her. Why should it?

They sat in the car with Radio One. A file of hikers appeared over the brow of the hill and strode past; they wore stout boots, orange anoraks and in their rucksacks there would be survival packs — tent and emergency rations. You could freeze to death up here.

Miranda wanted to get out. The cold air slapped them in the face. In her long dress, with the red boots and rabbit jacket, and her shawl round her head, she stood in the snow. At that moment the sun came out and fired the town below: all the watching windows to gold, the spires of churches, the silvered slates of the terrace roofs. She walked to the very edge of the scree, where the moors tumbled down, and he watched her.

They went down. He fed her hamburgers in a Wimpy where the drill-hall used to be, then they went to a pub for a whisky for him and she said she wouldn't mind a pasty. 'I've got to have a pee,' she said, 'it's the cold,' and while she was away Bradbury sat over his whisky and listened to the voices around him. Once he saw a man he thought he knew and touched him on the shoulder, but it was a stranger. Well. What had he expected? Welcome back, lad, have a black pudding?

'What's the joke?'

He shook his head.

Bradbury told her — not that she was interested (that was why he told her, because she wasn't interested?) — 'My father was a solicitor. We weren't grand but we were never poor. He grew flowers and cabbages and belonged to the naturalists' society. We always had our own house — quite small, one of those villas, but it wasn't a terrace and our garden was better than most. My mother taught me how to get away, then she didn't want me to leave.'

They climbed up Ropewalk to the castle (no one could budge that, anyway). The centre of the city, where the bus park used to be, had metamorphosised into an improbable piazza. He lost his bearings for a moment, then found the car again and they drove out to the house he had lived in as a child.

At first he thought he had made a mistake, taken a wrong turning, then he realised not. It was a waste and empty space. He sat hunched in the car. Change he'd armed himself for, but not obliteration.

Bradbury got out. It was sleeting now but he walked around bare-headed and here and there could find traces of garden walls, foundations, pavements, hearths, before which people had once sat; even a doorway, intact with frame, hinges and lintel — he pushed it open and beyond, through the door, was the girl laughing at him.

'Do come in,' she said. 'Wipe your feet.'

She danced around to keep warm. Bradbury called after her: 'Here it is! It was here, I think. No — there!' But it couldn't be. The rooms were too small? Or was that an illusion? Even rooms that stood, even new rooms — most of all, new rooms — looked small till you put the furniture in.

You think the houses of your childhood will stand for ever. It has nothing to do with whether you were unhappy there, or happy.

Miranda had found a bentwood kitchen chair. 'Do sit down,' she said. 'I'll put the kettle on.'

He stood, his hair rimed with sleet.

'Oh you,' she said. 'You and your past.'

Driving out of town again, they didn't speak. He concentrated on the slippery road, she curled up on the bench seat and seemed to sleep. They drew in at the same spot they had stopped the day before, above the valley. He got out to pee, closing the door quietly, not to wake her. When he got back she was standing outside the car, her duffle bag slung on her shoulder.

'I've never been to Glasgow,' she said. 'Don't fuss — there'll be a lorry.' She kissed his cold mouth, then she was off. A few minutes later a lorry going north stopped and picked her up.

Driving south, going home, Bradbury left the snow behind. When he stopped for a coffee, even in the darkness he was aware that the air and the earth were warmer here. Back in the car he twiddled the radio and found a symphony concert from the Festival Hall. He began to sing.

DAVID IRELAND

The Wild Colonial Boy

HE WAS an inoffensive statistic, who lived somewhere
on a graph of chance. His name was Martin Dangerfield,
but everyone called him Blue since his hair was red.

He'd come back when Australia's effort ended in
Vietnam, that place where hills sweat in the heat and
the sweat runs down in rivers. His name had come out
in the lottery and he'd gone over as a conscript and
come back minus a foot. But he'd never got over being
able to walk along holding an M16, and able, when
contacts were made, to fire it at humans. Like the rest
of us he'd shot birds, rabbits, foxes, and the lovable
kangaroo, but the ultimate privilege was aiming at
humans — with permission, under command! — and
squeezing that trigger. A towering feeling.

With a few beers in, we got the 'war-ies'. War stories.
When they heard the war words, guys nearby looked
him up and down and went to play pool. My old man
went to Korea and his father was in the Second World
War; neither of them would ever talk about it much.
And great-grandfather, when he got back from France
in 1920, threw his medals away. Everyone goes to the
wars, but no one likes to dwell on them later.

'I'm not saying it was such a good weapon. It made
a mighty hole, but a blade of grass would deflect the
bullet. The AK47 was much better,' he said enviously,
looking at old Hugh and Mick and me. I glanced round,

blindly, at the walls. Can walls despair? He was going to get very unpopular unless he could become a little more Australian, and forget.

Why should I care? I guess it was that he was one foot short. It would be nice if people could like him: he was going to be without that foot every day of his life.

It was Mick's turn to call the barmaid, Sharon, and order a round. He did all that.

A small black ant climbed up over the shiny steel lip of the bar and scouted round. It came near a sliver of bread crust and began pulling it. The crust was around three times the ant's length, but the ant was much stronger than the crust: it pulled easily. With a glorious abandon the little fellow tossed it back and forwards a number of times like a caber over its head, before settling down to the earnest business of the long haul back to the communal nest.

Mick's round came, he pushed our beers towards us, and left. As he was going, his name was called for pool.

When Martin Dangerfield mentioned his M16 I couldn't help saying, a bit quietly, 'Not wargasms, Blue. Not after all this time. People try to forget.'

Technically it's wrong to advise a guy what to do — you're supposed to let him do what he wants to do, then let him take what comes — but I did it.   .

'What do you mean, all this time? It's only a few years!' he said angrily. He didn't seem to realise people didn't talk about Vietnam any more.

'Have we got to bury it so quick? That's the trouble with this country — you do something for 'em and they get the shits with you! And you're never to mention it again.'

'Why now?' I said, compounding my social mistake.

'Why now?' he repeated, louder. 'Look at me! Where's my foot? It's gone *now*! Every day it's gone:

now! It'll always be now to me, the whole thing! It'll be now for ever!'

There was nothing to say to that, so I said nothing.

He took this as a sign that opposition had gone to ground, and went on. More quietly.

'Just the same, war is necessary, I don't care what the egg-heads say. Peace is silly talk, only those on top want peace. Those below want anything but peace, most of all they want change, with a chance to be on top. War's inevitable. Peace is like failure of nerve. I can say that, an ordinary foot soldier.'

Where did he get it? A short course on How Children Learn About War?

Then, without a blink, he changed direction and said, 'Myself, I don't indulge in war-ies. My mate Jeff, though, wasn't in, but he did himself a lot of good listening to me, then making up combat stories. He'd be up to his knees in spent grenade-pins and the chicks listening with mouths open.'

He smiled, and though no one else did, he seemed to feel approved. And buried his nose in the bubbles and froth of beer. He'd lost a foot, after all, why was I finding fault with him? I thought of him as still a kid, but he wasn't a kid; why shouldn't he talk about it as much as he wanted? Most young men who came back from there are so screwed up they can't talk about it to anyone that wasn't there.

'What was it like, fighting the Cong?' I asked.

'It wasn't fighting,' he said. 'The only contacts I ever had were from ambush. Sounds gutless, I know, but that's how it was. You'd be out there, you'd set up your weapon pit and so on, and just wait. Maybe nine o'clock at night, two in the morning, you'd hear little sounds, and presently there they'd be, old blokes or kids or anything, on bikes or on foot coming through the rubber trees. My first contact I loosed off sixteen shots. I knew I got one. Coming right towards me on a bike, no rifle or anything. In the morning I found him there, a hole through the middle and I'd blown his pack off and to pieces. We thought there were about five, but in the morning found it was nearer thirty.'

Old Hugh left off leaning against the red bar and went away to rest his leg. As he sat down I thought I heard him say something about a thin red line tipped with shit, not steel. But I could be wrong. The old are another race, sometimes.

We'd given Blue a send-off party before he went in. Someone said he'd be safe — any bullet would be sure to miss him by ten thousand metres. Not very kind, and not kindly meant. He wasn't a bad poor bastard, it's just that he wasn't anything in particular and people could take him or leave him. Mostly the latter.

'The second contact was in the early morning, about three. I couldn't see clearly, ambush again, and I fired off a burst on automatic at what I thought was a movement. In the morning I found I'd got him mainly in the head. Only the middle of his head was left. I'd stripped away both sides of his face, leaving the middle of the forehead, the nose and some jaw. It wasn't the best sight just before breakfast.'

I get vivid pictures in my head when I'm listening to people; I didn't like this picture. As a sort of defence against it I put a question to myself: Why, when one person orders, does another obey?

I couldn't answer it. It must be one of the central mysteries of the universe, though not necessarily for that reason.

'Did their colour bother you?' I asked.

'Funny you should say that. All the things you learn at school make you think you're going in there against little men, inferior weapons, like savages, and you expect to walk over them. The hardest thing to get used to was to see that, first, they were *so* small compared to us — a lot of them were kids — and second, their weapons were the same or better. It didn't seem fair, somehow. You know, the Empire bit, guns against spears like it's always been. When I saw the size of some of the kids I felt like a dead set cunt, then I realised I was a bigger target and that made it feel better. Just the same, it didn't feel right that they knew about guns and how to set explosives. Booby traps.'

He paused, and drank.

'I was surprised at all the buildings. I thought they lived in bush huts.'

'What buildings?'

'In the cities.'

'Well, never mind, Blue. Maybe the French built all those.'

'The French? What French?'

'They owned the country before the Yanks got there.'

'Did they?' But he seemed happier that the French built the buildings other than the bush huts.

'Anyway, it cost a lot of money,' he said, frowning seriously. 'Half a million to kill one Viet Cong. Half a billion to destroy one bridge, ninety-nine jets lost on it. You know,' he said confidentially, 'people get the wrong slant on wars like that. In a guerrilla war, the enemy is the people. To make progress, you flatten everything, get rid of their culture, break 'em up into individuals instead of groups, get 'em away from their family land, that demoralises 'em, get 'em into refugee camps where you can see 'em. The world doesn't need 'em, not people like that. Commies' — he used the American word rather than the Australian 'commos' — 'aiming to take over the world. Look at 'em. Satellites all round their borders, to protect themselves with other people's countries.'

'The Yanks have satellites right up to the commos' borders.'

'Yeah, that's to stop communism. If you've got a democratic way of life you've got to protect it.'

'I see your point,' I said.

We were standing near the beer taps. The noise in the pub had grown to its six o'clock peak. He had to shout to make me hear. Guys that came up and got their beer took a sip, and moved away.

Someone put money in and pushed buttons and the juke-box complained, like a baby crying in a gale:

> Alone in a town
> Without a phone
> No place to go
> No place to stay
> Friends all gone
> The last ones out
> Blew up the castles
> In the sky.

It was my favourite song for a while. There was a note plucked out of the guitar on the word 'castles' and lingering in the air after it — a beautiful note that struck right into me every time I heard it, piercing my life. It was as long as the horizon.

The total sound in the pub was so loud the singer and his guitar added up to just another noise. It didn't matter: there were no castles in the air round the Southern Cross pub. But I missed my special note.

I wondered to myself if the little black ant, alone with his burden and his prize, was meeting enemies on his way; and, if he had to drop the crust and fight, did he win?

Blue shouted in my ear. 'Of course, bad things were done. I heard of kids with napalm burns brought in by men of their village, and patrols from Da Nang shooting 'em, cutting off the men's heads for souvenir photographs, and cutting the kids' throats. They used to pose with the day's kill in heads in front of 'em.'

'That's a bit yuk,' I said. The most blood-thirsty warriors aren't always back home.

'They don't feel the same about dying as we do.'

'You mean they've got more guts?'

'Certainly not. They're more like animals. You've never heard animals scream for mercy, have you?'

'Pigs scream all the way to the abattoirs. I hear the truckload every morning past the golf course. Where I work.'

'Pigs are pigs,' he said derisively.

'They reckon they're intelligent.'

'Pigs are filthy,' he said, dismissing the subject. He looked at me as if I was about to pull a habit from my pants pocket and play with it.

'There was some dishonesty, too. Some would go out, kill a few in a contact, count 'em, bury 'em, then on the way back if they hadn't made their quota, they dug 'em up and counted 'em again.'

I'd like to have asked him my question about why one man takes orders from another, but I held my tongue.

'Over all, did you like the army?' I asked instead.

'I wish we'd got higher pay for danger, like the Yanks. Hostile-fire pay,' he said. 'No, I hated the army. Full of dead cunts. They'd yell out: C'mon you bastards! C'mon you dickhead cunts! when they wanted you to do something. And we weren't bastards, really. And not dickheads all the time, either.

'We got even with the army sometimes. When you got

hold of a Land-Rover you'd belt the guts out of it in first gear all the time. They'd whine like buggery, only last forty thousand miles. Would we double-declutch to second? Not on your nelly, no. Jam her into gear, bugger it. Or we'd go scrub bashing, knock over trees and all with their trucks. We weren't paying for it. Some of the motors were so good you could be doing sixty in forward gear, stick them in reverse and they'd go back-wards. Not a sound out of them.'

The soldier's revenge. I took a suck of beer as he continued.

'The army? No. Power goes to their heads. They'd have you cleaning their boots if they could. Mind you, you'd do it for the good officers, but there were only a few.'

'Do all those things worry you now?' He'd been out ten years, new artificial foot and all.

'I get a nightmare once in a while,' he said slowly.

'Not a daymare,' I said. It was the noise — that's my excuse.

'I get it in the daytime too,' he added, head down, looking into his glass. 'These little Asians, armed with our weapons, have got this white woman by the hair and a knife at her throat. One kid is grabbing her dress and crying and screaming, and the other is face down in the sand with an army boot on the back of his neck getting suffocated. I yell out to them to stop, but they calmly slit the woman's throat and suffocate the kid in the sand and someone grabs the other kid and throws it down and bashes it on the head with the butt of a rifle. And the woman looks up with the blood pumping out of her neck and calls, "Martin!" and it's Mum. And one of the kids is me.'

He swallowed his spit and seemed to have to chew it several times to get it down. He took a long drink of his beer and emptied it. I slid money across the red bar for the next round. Sharon saw the movement and pulled out two fresh schooner glasses. There was a reddish look to the outer rim of his eyes, but I couldn't see any excess liquid.

Some of the kids he used to play football with came in and waved from across the red bar, but didn't wish to disturb us. They were decent kids, but they must have picked that he'd had a few and was talking war and they wanted no part of being listeners. In this world things just aren't arranged for us to be kind to others.

Then he was saying, 'I was at Vung Tau, out on a routine daytime patrol single file and this mine went off behind me. I copped one hundred and ninety-two bits of shrapnel in the back of my legs and my bum and in two weeks I was back in the line. The poor bastard behind me disappeared. Wasn't even anything to shovel up. A month later I trod on one. Goodbye, foot. Every day in hospital when I woke up I remembered it all fresh and panicked when I couldn't find my foot.

'In another way it was a blessing.' Then caught himself. 'No, not that: it wasn't.' And explained. 'For months, ever since I got there, I could feel my death — I know it sounds funny — growing big inside me, bigger every day, thinking how I'd be: whether it was in bits, or shot, and where the holes would be, and which way I'd fall, and would they take me back home, or never find me, or would there be any of me left.

'Losing the foot, I knew I'd be out of it.' And he went on flatly, without emphasis.

'When I got back here in Sydney I saw all the people waiting to meet the boat, dressed in all sorts of colours, all shapes and sizes. This dazzle of colours. I thought I'd come back to a country of clowns. We were so used to the one colour all the time. And none of them had lost a foot. If you'd done it in a civvy job you'd get a few grand in compensation.

'That resentment was probably why I was always in trouble at first when I got back. They arrested me in hospital for swearing at the nurses and doctors.

'And now and then I go a bit funny and wake up looking for my foot and can't find it.'

I didn't mention that the last time he was drunk here at the Southern Cross late at night he was flailing about in the grass out the back towards Hunter's Creek, and his mind was back in the jungle looking for his lost foot, and he was crying.

'Did you find it? Over there, I mean?' I knew it was a lousy question.

'Didn't bother. Just sat down and waited to be picked up. Glad I hadn't disappeared like that other kid. But the main thing over there and here too was I was worried how to explain I'd lost my foot. I didn't want to look as if I was blaming the army, or the government, for us being there. I knew my family would be embarrassed. The main thing I thought of was I wouldn't be able to go to the beach. You know, it'd offend the birds. They wouldn't want to look round and there's some guy strapping on an artificial foot, or taking it off. I didn't want to be the one reminding them of the war when it was over and done. There's nothing as dead as a war after it's over. When you unstrap your foot and put a towel over it, it's like deliberately reminding people.'

'Did your nerves play up when you got back?' I found I wanted to ask questions now; it might be a long time before he'd talk about it again. It was just a feeling then, but I was right. That was six months ago and I've never heard him, or heard of him, talking 'war-ies' since.

'A bit. Depressed, lost my temper easily. Tried to

neck myself twice. This girl I was going with came to see me in hospital when I got back. I showed her the stump. She never came back. I get tied up inside so I'd like to be able to walk into a room relaxed and easy and suddenly shout out all the stuff inside me. Trouble is, I don't know just what I'd yell out.

'Still, the army's been great to me. This foot cost a lot of money and I get it free. If it breaks down I get another one.'

He stopped for a while, looking round at the pub full of drinkers. I had no way of knowing what he saw.

'Yet when I tried to get an allowance for running my car, like some of the others get, they knocked me back.

'Bloody doctors! You'd think the brass came out of their own pockets. I'm the one who had the foot off, not them! I'm the one who can't climb on a bus or a train very well, and fall over easy.'

'It's good to see a guy not bitter against the army,' I said. It wasn't a bright remark, but I'd just remembered then a time our club was playing at Marrickville and Blue was flattened in a late tackle. I was playing in the following game and helped him off the field. He didn't know where he was. When I put my arm round him to take the weight, and the trainer on the other side, he struggled till he freed himself, walking in the wrong direction. We led him off.

I felt so sorry for him now, never knowing when he'd fall over, I was about to put an arm round his neck and touch heads, not too gently, just for sympathy, and had to check myself. He didn't know about that sort of love — he'd have reared like a slighted stallion.

'The army's the best,' he continued, amazing me some more. 'You miss the action. The patrols, the danger, the feel of your weapon in your hands, all your mates.'

A man getting his beers nearby turned and looked.

'Would you go again. If,' and I looked down where his foot was.

'No worries. I'll say I would. Why dirty our own backyard when we can dirty theirs?'

It seemed to sum something up.

The man looking turned away, paid his money, got his change and took his beers outside to his mates without looking back.

'How did you get on with the long-hairs that made a fuss at the demos?' I asked him. Mine's long since cut, but I have a memory from those times of large blue men with big faces chasing grimed demonstrators across a park in Sydney. It's funny now.

'No time for the silly bastards. My hair was long before I went in the army, but they wouldn't talk to you once you had short back and sides. As if you were a different race. Apart from that, they were harmless. My old man was more down on 'em than I was. It's a free country; they can think what they like. I like long hair.'

As soon as he was out he'd grown a full beard, a magnificent Christ-beard: red. On the other hand it made him look remarkably like Ned Kelly, before the rope, the prison shave and the death mask.

'Your folks were happy to have you home, I bet.'

'Dad had gone a bit funny. They didn't tell me when I was over there, but he must have gone a bit peculiar when I left for overseas. And the foot made it worse.'

'What do you mean, funny?'

'Each day, all the years I've been back, he measures the growth of all the plants and trees at home. He buys packets and packets of seeds and plants and waters them, and seedlings from the nursery, there's no room to walk for plants and things growing. All the lawn's gone, filled up. He plants things everywhere there's a patch of soil.'

'Sounds harmless.'

'The neighbours want him put away. I won't have it. But he's spending a lot of his money now on wooden stakes as well as plants. He plants the stakes next to the trees and flowers and beans and tomatoes and notes down in books the growth every day. The place is a forest of measuring sticks.'

'What do you think did it?'

'I think it was me going to the war. He always supported Australia going to Vietnam but when it turned out I won a place in the lottery and it was me actually going over, and knowing how he taught me about fighting for your country when I was a boy and that I'd make sure I got into a combat unit and kill the enemy, not take an easy job at base, it was too much for him. It was all right as long as it wasn't me.'

'But what about the forest of stakes? What do you think it means?'

'Means?' he said. 'Nothing.'

'Everything means something.'

'Bullshit!' he answered confidently. 'That's the trouble with you civilians.' He was still an army man. 'Always looking to complicate things, mess everything up with words, words.'

He took a long suck and drained his glass.

'Look. I went to the war: fact. My Dad's gone funny: fact. I lost a foot: fact. You don't need words. Words are a drug. If the armed forces had had their way, and no words, we'd have won. War is for the fighting men. We'd have ridden right over the bastards.'

'Come off it. You couldn't have won in ten *more* years. They had the wood on you. They had you stuffed and burnt. It was their country. You were tourists.'

I don't know why anyone won. All I know is I

wouldn't like foreign soldiers here in Australia and I wouldn't mind fighting to get rid of them. I guess patriotism is a dirty word in our part of the world: the thing is it's not at all a dirty word in other countries.

He looked at me as if I was a Communist in a tunnel and he was one of the good guys poised with a flame-thrower. Then looked away, across the bar into the street, where the endless traffic, like units of time, transported countless other lives past our lives. Even if you ran out the door, once they'd gone past there was no trace of them, nothing to say who they were.

I stood there a bit, looking for patterns in the froth on my glass after the beer was gone.

When I looked up *he* was gone.

I thought of the little black ant with its crust; of the pity and the pain of the tiny creature; its courage, its heroic efforts: coming from nothing and going to nothing.

Someone called my name for a game of pool. I went over and tossed for break. As I lined up the white on an edge of the triangle of coloured balls I found I was aiming to hit one of the reds. One thing he hadn't mentioned, one word he hadn't said: blood. I straightened, looking round for my beer, but of course I'd finished it.

Martin Dangerfield was an inoffensive bubble who lived somewhere on an empty glass.

GILLIAN TINDALL

Victory

MARY SPENCER-BYRD had been elected on to the
Cemetery Committee for the same reason that she was
elected on to a number of local committees: she was
an energetic single woman of advancing years with no
job, no apparent disabilities and no evident worries. She
was also — though most of her fellow committee
members would have refrained from stating the fact
baldly in these democratic days — a member by birth of
the class which has traditionally provided people to sit
on parish councils and Benches, to run civic societies
and conservation groups and fund-raising campaigns, to
impede the opening of new motorways and to prevent
the closure of old footpaths, and in general to referee
the creaking and complex machinery of English society
over its own particular territory.

Mary's territory was the old village of Woodgate some
nine miles from central London, around which have
grown since the First World War the great suburbs of
Woodgate East, Woodstow and Hayling. Mary could
remember when Woodgate village green, which was now
smoothly mown and protected by white posts and
chains and flower-beds, had had sheep grazing on it. She
could remember when there were open fields between
Woodgate and the newly opened Underground line at
Hayling: the Tube had stopped there in those days. She
could remember when Mr Lucas had done his own

butchering in the yard behind his bloody, fly-infested shop in the narrowly picturesque High Street: today the street's picturesqueness had been carefully preserved, though marred by the traffic that every day almost clogged it, but 'Mr Lucas's' (as she still called it in her mind) sold cotton clothes in Provencal prints, hand-made jewellery, and cloth bags encrusted with peasant embroidery done in factories near Bombay.

She could also remember when all the white stuccoed houses round the green, and all the big red-brick ones down Chestnut Avenue and The Grove that were now occupied by bankers or lawyers or well-known actors, or divided into flats, had belonged to old Woodgate families including her own. But she did not often refer to those times, for she had long ago determined that no one should ever class her as a silly old dear yearning for a past that would never return. In any case, some of these new people (she still secretly thought of them as 'new', even the families who had moved there in the nineteen twenties and thirties as London expanded) were quite splendid: well-educated, public-spirited, most capable and influential. Woodgate had certainly been fortunate, for without them to keep an eye on things the state of the village today might have been very different. Whenever Mary drove down to Hayling to Marks & Spencer's or Sainsbury's, or over through Woodstow and the new housing estates there on the way to see her sister in Buckinghamshire, she shuddered inwardly to think of the tide of uncaring, wanton change that might so easily have swamped Woodgate itself had she and all the other concerned people been less vigilant all these years. . . .

Why, without their presence the Cemetery Committee would never have been set up. What would have happened to the wonderful old place, all twenty-one acres of elaborate sculptury set now, for the most part, in dense undergrowth, if the residents of Woodgate Village had not been on the alert in the nineteen sixties when the Cemetery Company had finally decomposed into liquidation? — as the chairman of the Committee had so amusingly put it. Apparently a cemetery that was too full for any new graves did not represent an asset but, rather, a formidable liability: maintenance costs had risen and risen and the sums of money that families like the Spencer-Byrds had covenanted long ago to have their family plots cared for 'in perpetuity' had been rendered derisory through time and inflation. Funny to think that once, besides being one of the most fashionable places in the London area for burial, the place had also been a 'very sound investment'. Mary's own grandfather had had shares in it, and he had been an astute investor, as Mary's own continuing private income, even in these difficult times, testified. She sometimes contemplated with a kind of placid wonder the fact that her present modest comfort derived from fatherly and grandfatherly foresight from over a hundred years ago. Good things *could* last, given care and watchfulness. . . . A heritage. . . . For the benefit of future generations. . . . (And similar phrases.)

That was what the cemetery was also. And goodness knows what horrors of municipal good intentions the local borough council would have perpetrated when the cemetery came under their reluctant charge had it not been for herself and the rest of the Committee stepping into the breech! In the course of many years' sterling work on committees (always 'sterling' in votes of thanks) Mary had imbided a patchy legal knowledge, and she was aware that no powers, short of a special Act of Parliament, could have enabled the council to use the place for a new housing development, as the more vociferous and brutish councillors had apparently hoped. But their planning department could have wrought its own subtle desecration: wholesale stone removal . . . cement paths . . . municipal daffodils . . . a children's playground, forever being vandalised . . . Disliking children, she shuddered inwardly; she had been a spectator for many decades of the doctrinaire crassness of local councils. She had sometimes wondered if she ought not to stand for the council herself, to help combat their stupidity at close quarters, but she felt (as she told her friends) that she really could not have *endured* the company of some of those people from Hayling and East Woodgate. . . . The present Committee, of course, was a very different affair, being largely composed of Woodgate Village people with only a few docile outsiders to represent other interests.

They were talking, this evening, about the Dinshaw-Thacker grave: Item 5 on the agenda. In fact it seemed to have been an item on the agenda at every meeting for at least a year, and although they had had much encouraging discussion nothing had actually been decided. J. G. Dinshaw-Thacker, the famous Indian cricketer, had died of pneumonia in 1909 on his first and only visit to London, and had been buried by a sorrowing multitude in the cemetery whose comprehensively non-denominational nature was well known. The secretary was of the opinion that the M.C.C., with whom he said he was in 'close correspondence', might be persuaded to stump up a few hundred to restore the monument — a giant marble wicket, bowled by an enormous ball. But Mr Rammage the treasurer, who tended to cast himself in the role of hard-headed businessman and shatterer of illusions, scoffed at this: the M.C.C. wouldn't waste their funds on the memory of a foreigner, he said, however illustrious; Dinshaw-

Thacker's own lot should be persuaded to divvy up. After all, there was no shortage of them these days. Hayling was full of 'em.

The chairman, with a slightly anxious glance at Mr Rammage, who did tend to get going rather, said that this was certainly an idea. Perhaps one of them should approach the leader of the London Hindu community, whomsoever that might be?

'But Dinshaw-Thacker was a Parsee,' said Mr Tobin, a rather colourless architect who, however, occasionally knew things. Mary wondered fleetingly if he had been born in India. She glanced at his finger-nails.

'Does that make a difference?'

'If he'd been a Hindu he wouldn't have been buried anyway. Hindus burn their dead. Actually Parsees are supposed to put their dead in roofless towers to be pecked to bits by vultures — towers of silence, they're called. But I suppose there weren't any of those in London. . . . Probably still aren't.'

'And not many vultures,' said a woman member of the Committee with a nervous giggle.

Rammage snorted. 'Disgusting. I should think not. How they can, beats me.'

But is it disgusting? thought Mary. Is it really any more disgusting than putting someone to rot in a varnished box underground? And how can people do that, when they really think — *really* think — what it means? Most people have no imagination, and just as well.

Her mind slid back on an accustomed track to her own family grave, not very far from Dinshaw-Thacker's as it happened, on the western side of the cemetery. Her grandparents were there, and her parents, but for some reason she never contemplated their continuing presence in that place, perhaps partly on account of a vestigial childhood belief that they were 'really' in heaven. The only person she felt to be in the grave was her brother Nigel. When her skimming imagination stripped away the layers — the cow parsley and nettles first, then the stone, then the earth, then the varnished lid — it was Nigel who lay revealed to her.

She had never mentioned to anyone on the Committee that she had this personal stake in the cemetery, almost a physical link. . . . She would rather keep all that side of things out of their pleasant meetings. She told herself that it had never been her policy to mix business and private matters. The grave-plot, though large and with room still to spare, was not a distinctive one and was fortunately in the most deeply wooded part. The cemetery records had been destroyed by a timely incendiary bomb near London Wall in 1940.

They were still on Dinshaw-Thacker. Someone was suggesting approaching the Calcutta Cricket Club for financial support. Mr Tobin, having made his unusual contribution, had apparently lost interest. He was sketching a nice little eighteenth-century doorway in the margin of the agenda, carefully shading the fanlight. She watched with pleasure as he began to add a house round it.

Nigel had talked of being an architect, as he had talked of many things that, in the event, he had not had time to accomplish. 'Such a gifted, promising boy,' an old friend of the family had written to their father after Nigel had been killed in that terrible car-crash. Their father had kept that letter till his own death, but afterwards, clearing out the family house, she had burnt it. She remembered the emotions with which she had watched it flame. *Hindus burn their dead*. It hadn't made any difference, though.

She must have missed something, for they were

apparently on to Item 6a now, the mortuary chapel, an unsafe structure whose fate hung, in several senses, in the balance. The council wanted to demolish it; the D. of E., however, were thought to favour its restoration on historical grounds. Reassured that this delicate balance showed, for the moment, no sign of being upset, Mary returned to her private, obsessing theme.

One reason why she had never mentioned in committee that Nigel (and her parents of course) were in the cemetery was that the people round the table would misunderstand. With a quickness born of an under-exercised intelligence and a lifetime of reading novels, she could see all too clearly how *they* would see it: the lonely but plucky old maid, still after fifty years mourning her only brother . . . the shared childhood . . . the young life cut short . . . the Golden Boy in his red roadster . . . the slim volume of poetry he had published only the year before . . . the humorous sketches . . . the heartbroken testimonials from godparents, teachers and old school-friends. . . . Even the fact that he had died with a girl in the car who was unknown to anyone but who proved to be the daughter of a publican in Hayling might, at a distance of fifty years, be interpreted as a poignant and romantic circumstances . . . young love . . . the runaway passion that brooked no denying. . . .

Mary made a face and consciously pulled herself together. That was really a little too much: she never read *that* sort of novel, after all. Young love indeed! You really were getting old when you assumed young love to be naturally romantic and pure. She recalled the couples from the East Woodgate Comprehensive School who were said to break into the cemetery at night and 'copulate' on the graves, and again she felt that bracing charge of emotion she had felt when she burnt the letter Father had kept.

But it was no good. He would just have laughed. His throat, rising from a white cricket shirt, elongated and almost girlish as in the pastel sketch of him that had been in Mother's bedroom. Young for ever. . . . Dust to dust. How sorry the Committee would be if they knew that so much youth and strength and gaiety had just been put away under the ground. It would not occur to them to take any other view.

Young for ever. But he had only been a year younger than she. Now he would be a man past middle age, slow and craven, perhaps, like the rest of them round this table. She looked at their receding hair or frankly bald heads, at their bloodshot eyes and weathered cheeks, at their jowls and their stringy necks and at the liver-coloured patches on their hands. And her train of thought ended, as it always ended, in a sense of frustration, the realisation once again that age shall not wither Nigel nor the years condemn. . . . Young for ever.

The secretary was reading out some estimates for the repair of the boundary walls (Item 6b). The sums of money sounded absurdly enormous. Surely it couldn't cost all that just to rebuild some brickwork? But the several architects present appeared to be contemplating the sums with placidity, even with complacence. Of course the architect's fee was normally, or so she understood, a percentage of the total costs. . . . But no, it was out of the question to think of any of the Committee in that light: people of the highest probity and scruple all of them. All the same, no wonder architects seemed to earn a lot.

Nigel would no doubt have earned a lot — if his ideas about architecture had ever come to anything. In fact, now she came to think about it, it might have been the ideal occupation for him, with his many gifts: his enterprise, his flair for making strangers like him, his quickness at sensing any new trend, his talent for sketching . . . .

. . . His fondness for grandiose schemes at other people's expense, his glib virtuosity, his weakness for anything new and contempt for anything old, his essential destructiveness. *How* he would have enjoyed destroying the old cemetery, and indeed the whole of Woodgate Village, and putting other things in their place. Yes, in the twentieth century, architecture or town planning would have been a very suitable occupation for him.

(Mr Rammage was remarking that the council might be persuaded to shell out more money for the boundary walls if a big enough stink about break-ins and vandalism were raised in the local Press. Come to that, the national Press might stir their stumps if they thought the story was juicy enough. At this, several people round the table looked nervous, and one lady remarked rather sharply after a slight pause that surely lurid publicity was the *last* thing they wanted?)

Cruel, thought Mary relentlessly: he was cruel, he despised us all, even Father. The fights they used to have. . . . And the way he bullied me all through our childhood and teens, even though he was the younger, demonstrating to me over and over and over again that he was the clever one, the master, and that I was a poor, muddle-headed, sentimental creature incapable of logical thought or efficient action. Well, Nigel, I've spent my life proving that you were wrong: I've turned myself, over the decades, into efficient, sensible Miss Spencer-Byrd. I never married the flabby fool you predicted for me. I've long ago given up the ready tears which you portrayed again and again in those cruel, beastly drawings you used to do. You were wrong, Nigel. In spite of all your cleverness you were wrong, and I have proved it.

The last thing he ever said to me, the very last thing as he was dressing to go out that night, was: 'Mary, if you tell the parents about Dolly I'll make damn sure you're sorry. I'm warning you!' And I didn't tell, because I was a coward in those days, and when the police came at midnight and told us about the crash my first thought was: *Who's sorry now?* They were the words of a popular song then, and they fitted so perfectly.

But of course the dead aren't sorry, because they don't know enough to be. It's time and knowledge that make you sorry about things, and the dead are safe from time and knowledge. The dead are secure.

How he would hate the idea that he's just one more body in a picturesque old graveyard which no one must touch or alter! I tell myself that. . . . And yet, just as when I burnt that fulsome, sentimental letter about him, I don't feel that much triumph; I don't feel I have really got the better of him. For he's young and he's dead and therefore beyond reach. You won, Nigel, you won — though almost every day in the last fifty years I have done some little thing or other in an attempt to prove to myself that you did not. *'Where is death's sting? Where, grave, thy victory?'* When grandfather Spencer had that carved on the stone for his wife in 1882 he can never have imagined what a bitter interpretation the words might have.

(The estimates for the boundary walls were still being discussed. The general feeling of the meeting was that some work must be done soon, even of a provisional nature, in view of the 'incursions' by tramps and teenagers. Mr Rammage also mentioned the words ' . . . like a public lavatory' in tones of explosive disgust.)

Nigel would have enjoyed baiting Mr Rammage.

Come to that, he would have enjoyed what was happening in the cemetery these days; it was just the sort of sordid, distressing thing that he found funny. It must be stopped. Copulating on the graves, indeed! He'd have drawn dirty pictures of it. That private sketch-book of his I found after his death. . . .

She raised her hand:

'Mr Chairman, I should like to endorse most strongly this recommendation about work being done *pro tem.* to make the cemetery more secure. After all, apart from the question of possible damage to monuments, I feel that it is our first duty to ensure that the peaceful character of the place is maintained. Surely we owe that at least to the dead — before we can begin to consider the needs of the living?'

The murmur of acquiescence round the table reassured her.

ELIZABETH TROOP

On Hearing the First Gigli in Spring

IT WAS just after the war when we heard he was visiting the town. I couldn't believe it. Gigli. A famous tenor, coming *there*. Maxine, my sister, was scornful. 'A fat old singer, what's the fuss? If it was Frankie Sinatra I could understand it. Or Perry Como. But *him*?'

We only had two classical records — one was Gigli singing 'Your tiny hand is frozen', the other Solomon playing Tchaikovsky's First Piano Concerto. These recordings summed up a whole world for me, far removed from the American Forces' Network patter that beamed out from the loudspeaker — brown, bakelite-ribbed — we rented from Rediffusion at one and sixpence a week.

My mother and father had been great opera buffs when they first married, going as far as Manchester to hear *Bohème* and *Tosca* and my father's favourite, *The Mastersingers*. The Carl Rosa visited once, and, I suppose as a form of homage to those old days, my mother took me to *Butterfly*, but I was too young, and had to go out during the love duet to do a wee-wee.

Maxine, the local dancing-class star and beauty (auburn hair without the customary freckles), announced to me that classical music was dreary, that I liked it only because it made me superior; it was like my drawing. I spent hours copying the Great Paintings from the Children's Encyclopaedia, intending to become the first truly great female artist. 'You are wasting your time,' Maxine said, 'for it is a well-known fact that no woman has ever been, or will ever be, a Great Artist.' Maxine knew more well-known facts than anyone in history. I ignored her, and her friends. They were always trying to learn the words of the new songs they heard on A.F.N. Munich, but they never caught up. What was the point of singing 'Chloe' like Spike Jones and his City Slickers? I couldn't see it. I retaliated by playing Gigli at full blast. 'You should know it's had it, that type of music,' said Maxine. 'How old are you, twelve? You behave as if you were ninety.'

I worried about this; she was often right, with her well-known facts. She was one of those who had it all taped. Her hair never tangled in knots so that Mother couldn't get it sorted out without screams of pain, it hung down curly and red like a Burne-Jones painting. She liked school dinners. Boys never teased her, and she never had a secret desire to be one. She even got on with older men, the ones who have not gone away to the war. Uncles and shopkeepers too old to enlist, or the disabled in some way; she talked to them and they blossomed. But she never truly missed our Dad, or did Mum's hair in a new style, or took her off to see Bette Davis to cheer her up. I did those. So it seemed to me that perhaps things got shared out equally; she got all the exterior perks and I the interior ones, and so it turned out, later on.

I cycled down to the Royal Opera House, which rarely housed opera, and asked about Gigli tickets. I was too early. It was three months ahead. They were surprised I even knew about it. I was relieved in a way that it was so far in the future; I had seen the price list pinned in the box office — I would have to see about getting enough money together to take myself and

Mother. It would be unthinkable not to get to see him, after all that fuss in front of Maxine and Co.

Wobbling home in the summer traffic I tried to calculate how to earn small amounts of cash. Maxine earned quite a bit working in a guest-house owned by the mother of a friend, but there wouldn't be anything like that for me. She wouldn't lend any either — it was a well-known fact that W. Shakespeare had said 'Neither a borrower nor a lender be. . . .' She charmed the visitors she waited on, sometimes getting as much as half-a-crown tip at the end of the week. She was saving it all to go to Hollywood. Though some of it was spent on her so-called natural beauty. Special shampoos for instance. 'No "Friday night is Amami night" for her,' said my mother. I watched Maxine put creams on her unlined face and slices of cucumber over her unpuffed eyes. 'You look like a salad,' I said. 'The cream is the mayonnaise.' I told her they would soon be eating her up, at Mrs Roger's boarding-house. 'She gives such small portions — she keeps saying "There's a war on" — even though it's over.'

'Don't think some of them wouldn't like to — eat me up, that is,' Maxine said, mysterious as ever. I hated it when she tried on the mystery. After all, we knew each other as well as two sisters who shared a bedroom could; I knew she was scared of the dark, couldn't sleep on her back without snoring. She knew I cried in my sleep and could not go off unless I had a portion of an old wool blanket tucked in my forefinger. We knew (I thought) everything about each other, the smells, the moods, the hatreds, the longings. So where did she get this mysterious other knowledge? She was never out of my orbit. I made the mistake, then as later, of thinking unconscious selves were revealed by habit, by laziness. (It seems funny to me when I see her now, heavy and tranquillised, that the slim, know-it-all Maxine is lurking in there — has been through two broken marriages and a nervous breakdown — the charismatic star of my childhood and, I suppose, her own.)

My mother expressed interest, mild interest, in hearing Gigli. It was enough to set me going. She was decorating the front double bedroom, with the intention of letting it out to summer visitors, to make some cash. It was always short since Father died. She wanted Maxine to leave the Grammar School and take a secretarial course. All those things were on her mind. Seeing Gigli would be a miracle for her, I knew that. But she was too jaded to believe that. 'You'll never afford it,' was all she said. How could neither of them see how important it was — *he* was bothering to visit this stupid town? For me it was as if it had suddenly sprung to life on the map. Nowhere-in-particular was *somewhere*.

I got a job in a ceramic studio, Saturdays. There was an advertisement in the evening paper: 'Junior wanted, art studio.' My heart leapt. I might even be taking the first steps towards becoming the first female Leonardo da Vinci. By the time Gigli came I might be famous myself. Mr Kowalski did not want to take me on. He eyed me suspiciously, in my navy gymslip and black stockings. 'I can do it,' I said, looking at the line of girls, none of them much older than me, but all already workers. They were painting spots on the turbans of ceramic negresses. Wall plaques of great ugliness.

Red spots on yellow. It made me cringe. I wasn't fast enough, either, tongue sticking out, trying to emulate the other girls, who ignored me. I tried on my second Saturday to get Mr Kowalski to change the colours, do multi-coloured spots. 'Cheek,' I heard one of the girls say. It would have been more trouble. As it was, the negresses spun down the line of girls as fast as they would have done in a factory assembly — until they came to me. 'Don't take so much care; you aren't painting the Sistine Chapel,' said Mr Kowalski. I was surprised he'd heard of it. 'Who hangs these on the wall?' I asked him, all innocent disbelief. 'Lots of people do.' I had a lot to learn about the human race.

I lasted four weeks, then was fired for being too slow. My first failure. Artistic integrity, I told myself. I was too good for them.

Judy was my next hope. A wire-haired terrier, she'd been given to me by the lady next door when she moved. I loved that dog to distraction. I considered, after examining her pedigree, that she could be shown. Dog shows went on all the time — big money would be won. I tried to train her; walking her around in circles in the back yard, telling her to 'Heel!' She took no notice. She was a prime specimen; I could just see her strutting about the ring at the local show. Mr Fernald, show breeder and dog clipper, who did Judy every six weeks, told me it was an impossible dream. One: she was too old, and fat, being fed from family scraps. Two: her ears were not quite right. Instead of turning over delicately at the ends like all other fox terriers, they stuck up like a rabbit's — hadn't I noticed that? I had, but didn't suppose it was *that* important. It turned out it was. 'She were born like it. The runt of the litter, most likely.' For a while I attempted to do something about her ears. I stuck Elastoplast over the tips, to weight them down. When this didn't work I put in tiny beach pebbles, for added incentive. They stuck up immediately the plaster was removed. Judy began to run when she saw me coming. 'She's only good for breeding,' said Mr Fernald. 'Leave her ears alone. It's cruel.'

'How can I get her mated? She's on heat.' Mr Fernald blushed. I knew he had a good stud dog. I watched him trim Judy on his neat green lawn. Her beard stuck out, powdered and cheerful. She had a lovely nature.

'You couldn't bring her to stud. It wouldn't be right, a young lass like you.' I told him I knew what went on. 'Would my sister do — she's . . . twenty? ' I lied.

I wondered if Mr Fernald knew Maxine was only sixteen. He didn't say. He probably fancied Maxine, for he agreed. 'She should produce a nice little litter. I'll mate her with Bobby.' I told him I couldn't pay the stud fee. He said he'd take the pick of the litter; it was often done that way.

Judy, pregnant, waddled along the beach with me and Maxine. 'How long now?' Maxine asked. 'Poor little thing,' she said; she who had never shown the slightest interest in Judy before. 'Fancy having to bear pups for a fat Italian tenor.' I ignored her. She hadn't liked going along for the mating session, but had been mollified by the fact that Mr Fernald was bowled over by her beauty and had tried to get her to go to the pub on Sunday morning. Maxine had seen the moon face of Mrs Fernald peering out of the upper window, and had refused.

'A couple of weeks,' I said. Mr Fernald told me I could get deposits on the pups, if they looked all right, from the prospective buyers, which would enable me to book the tickets on the day of issue. Judy fainted once. She was a bit old to be starting breeding, said the vet.

I prepared a long banana crate with straw and installed her in there. She had begun sitting down suddenly and looking surprised. I assumed something was up. She lay in the box, panting and heaving, under the kitchen table. Finally I heard tiny mouse-like squeaks, and saw three ratty little creatures gnawing at Judy's dugs. 'Come on, old girl,' I said. 'Three puppies is not enough. Most of your kind have five or six.'

Maxine slammed out at that. In some ways she was more soft-hearted than I. She had managed to persuade me to give her half the price of one of the pups as a fee for going to the breeding session. She wasn't that daft.

I was amazed how quickly the little creatures cottoned on to what life was all about. After a day or so they made their way down to the other end of the box to perform their natural functions. Judy had a love—hate relationship with them, like most mothers. They bugged her constantly, attaching themselves to her nipples whenever they were within suckling distance. 'She's like an ever-open milk bar,' said Maxine. 'I won't ever go through that.'

Mr Fernald came and made his choice, the largest and fittest dog. He examined the ears carefully. They were all right. I breathed a sigh of relief. The smallest one, the one Maxine had named 'Frankie' after the singing bean-pole, showed signs of inheriting Judy's stick-up ears. 'You'll have to charge less for that one,' said Mr Fernald. 'Nature's revenge,' said Maxine. The third pup was a bitch, and you got less for a bitch. Nature's revenge again, I supposed. I had hoped to buy a new dress and a pair of high-heeled shoes for the concert but now the profits were dwindling. I would probably just manage the tickets.

The tickets nestled in my drawer, next to the new high heels. I had managed both, because Mr Kowalski had called me back for a couple of Saturdays. One of his girls had 'flu. I was promoted to flying ducks; more classy really. The two puppies I had to sell went like hot cakes. I got the deposits without any trouble. I couldn't let them go until they were six weeks old — they now ate like little horses. Judy spent her life trying to avoid them. Mr Fernald took his early.

I tried on Maxine's extensive wardrobe. I was too fat; puppy fat, they called it. She thought that funny. Mother altered one for me; a pink effort, with a bow on the hip. It looked awful. I resemble a pork sausage, I said to my reflection. Gigli would never notice a person like that.

Maxine knew my thoughts, as usual. 'I suppose you think he is going to spot you in the audience. And him old enough to be your grandfather. You should take me with you. I'm sure to be noticed.' True. But she wouldn't come. Bored blue, she'd be. Said so in no uncertain terms. 'You look forty-five in that,' she cried as she went off to the pictures. Kind sister. 'You're waddling like a ruptured duck,' said my mother as we rushed for the tram. 'It must be those ridiculous shoes.' Families. They killed all joy.

The Royal Opera House didn't usually have opera, but variety shows and touring plays. Vivien Leigh had once come in *The Doctor's Dilemma*, but nobody as exalted as Gigli, not as far as I could remember.

It was full, of course, being a Gala Occasion. The Mayor and Corporation, all mothballs and corsages. Mother held herself very straight; she puffed as we ascended to the Circle. She had only finished decorating the bedroom hours before. We were bang in the middle of the row, and it was very hot. I hoped I would be able to stand it. Such excitement was being generated. I couldn't make out if everybody felt it, or if it was just me.

He came on. There was just a giant grand piano, a plant, the pianist and him. Tumultuous applause. I pinched myself to make sure I was there. The liquid voice soared out above the heads, above the scattered notes of the piano. I didn't know the song, or aria, and had forgotten to read it up in the programme. I felt far

away, as if I wasn't there at all. I thought of the squirm-
ing puppies, Frankie and Mimi, and of Maxine at the
pictures. More applause. I'd missed that one. I must
concentrate. I began to sweat. How strange, we were all
sitting here, listening to this one man. Maxine had said
he was old, she was right. He was sweating too, mopping
his brow after each song. Perhaps we felt it more deeply,
he and I, because we were both artists. I thought of the
negresses and the flying ducks. I wasn't an artist. Not
yet. I began to bite my nails. My mother slapped my
hand, and the man behind said, 'Ssh.' Gigli began 'Your
tiny hand is frozen'. I waited for the scratch, thinking I
was at home with the old gramophone. But of course, it
wasn't there. I jumped out of my skin at the shouts of
'Bravo'. How was it all these people behaved as if they
knew him too? 'You're not feeling sick, are you?' said
my mother. If I was she would take me out. Honestly,
I thought. You'd think *she* had got the tickets.

The interval. She looked tired, and there was a streak
of paint on the front of her hair where the enamel had
brushed her. It made her look old.

'No, I don't want an ice-cream,' I said, furious at the
thought. How could they all guzzle at the bar that way,
while *he* was going through agonies to bring his artistry
to them? We went back to our seats. Someone tapped
Mother on the shoulder. 'Forgive me, but could you
keep your little girl still? She keeps moving about. . . .'
My mother nodded, ashamed. The man sat back,
perusing his programme.

I stared hard as it began again; determined to store it
all away, for it might never happen again. It was slipping
away while I tried to hold on to it. My mother fanned
me with the programme, feeling my tension, as mothers
do. 'Stop it,' I hissed. 'Oh *really*,' cursed the man behind
us.

'Encore,' they all shouted. 'Bravo.' He sang two light songs for encores. I began to relax. Too late. It was over. I clapped until my palms ached. Everyone was getting their things, shuffling out. If it had begun now I would have taken it all in, every scrap. It was just that I wasn't used to this sort of thing. 'Do you want to go back?' said my mother. 'Backstage to get his autograph? On your programme?' 'Oh no,' I breathed. 'I couldn't do that.' I wanted to go home.

The man who had been behind us came up. My mother looked frightened. I could see she was preparing some line of defence. 'I'm sorry if we were fidgety,' she said. I looked daggers at him. 'Not at all,' he said. 'I was wondering if you would like to have a drink, discuss the concert. It was beautiful, wasn't it?' My mother agreed. She was looking at him, and then at me. 'I don't know,' she said. She had two little spots of colour on her cheeks, a sign she was excited. 'You go along,' I said. 'I'll go back on the tram. Think about the music. . . .'

They went off. He was chattering, nineteen to the dozen. She was clinging to his arm, looking up at him. She still looked scared. I had managed to get the programme out of her clenched hand. She was that nervous, getting a date after all these years.

I looked at the picture of Gigli in the programme as the tram clanked along. He looked more available in picture form than he had on that stage. Perhaps that was because I'd had to share him with all those people in the hall. I could pin the picture on my own wall. If Maxine would let me, that is.

I'd found it difficult getting up the stairs of the double-decker tram in my new high heels. I was frozen, not having worn a coat. I wondered what Gigli had made of Blackpool. Just another town to him, I supposed. The sea was a silver mass in the dark. I could hear it heaving and thudding as it always did. I was fond of the sea. How could people just go home, after that? Perhaps it was better, the way they were. They had taken it all in; I hadn't. I couldn't remember a note. The whole experience had been a dream. I shivered. There was nothing to look forward to now. Except becoming a world-famous artist. Oh, that.

Maxine was wrestling with a man on the studio couch when I got in. It was Mr Fernald. 'How was it?' she was keen to know, smoothing down her skirt. 'Disappointing,' I said, picking up Mimi, and kissing her on her warm belly. 'Told you it would be,' she said, touching up her lipstick.

Judy wagged a welcome at me. Poor thing. She'd done her bit. I wished in a way I had decided to keep one of the puppies. 'Goodnight, then,' I said. 'Mother's gone to the pub with a friend.'

Upstairs I put the programme and the torn ticket stub in my drawer, beneath the newspaper lining, so that Maxine wouldn't see them. I put on the record. Gigli sang, as always: 'Che gelida manina. . . .'

'Turn that row off,' shouted Maxine. I ignored her.

It was all coming back to me now. I was making it mine.

JOHN WAIN

The Snowman Maker

AS SOON AS Madame Stroehmann had given Danièle
her breakfast (milky coffee, crisp rolls and black cherry
jam with plenty of pure creamy butter to give the child
her proteins and fats), she agreed to let her go outside
and play. As a rule she made Danièle stay indoors until
the sun had warmed the air a little. The Alpine nights
were freezing, and the wall of mountains kept the sun
away from village-level until — well, it depended where
your chalet was situated. The mountains were like a row
of huge white teeth — known, indeed, as *Les Dents du
Midi* — and here and there was a tooth missing, or an
irregularity, that allowed a wedge of sunlight to strike
down to the lower slopes, so that one cluster of wooden
houses would be lit and warmed by the sun while
others, fifty yards away, would have to wait out another
two hours of cold shadow. (And of course on the other
side of the valley there were chalets, sometimes used for
storage and sometimes as the homes of poor people who
had failed to make their way in life, that had no sun at
all on a winter's day; between September and April they
stood in permanent cold and gloom, as if even among so
much natural beauty there were fore-ordained slums
created by the pattern of light and shade.)

The Stroehmanns' chalet stood in one of the most
favoured spots, getting the full beams of the sun well
ahead of most of the village. That was why the site had

been expensive, but when Herr Stroehmann decided that an Alpine retreat was a necessity for his family and it was absurd to go on renting them and putting money into the pockets of landlords, he put his good solid money where his good solid decisions were. Herr Stroehmann was only a young man, still on the easy side of thirty-five, but he was well trusted and well favoured in the big organisation he worked for, and money was coming his way and would keep on coming.

He was Herr Stroehmann but his wife was Madame. When he had fallen in love with her and begged her very hard and very repeatedly to become his wife, she had demurred at first on the grounds that she was very much a French Swiss and he very much a German Swiss. In the *Suisse Romande* we do things differently, she had said to him. There will always be barriers to communication. As well marry a Ticinese.

He had considered the matter carefully (he considered every matter carefully), and then come back with the answer. His firm had a branch in Geneva. He would move there, and as far as possible adapt to French-Swiss ways. (Except that he would be Herr Stroehmann. Somehow he knew he could not be Monsieur.) As his wife, she would live among her accustomed scenes and accustomed ways, and any children with whom they might be blessed would be brought up in the French-Swiss way. He, in short, would make all the adaptations and give all the ground, if she would only consent to be Frau Stroehmann — he begged her pardon, Madame.

She was finally convinced, captivated indeed, by this magnificent practical proof of devotion and unselfishness. So here she was now, watching the strong February sunlight descending minute by minute the wide slope of shadowed snow towards their chalet. Little Danièle had trotted up the hillside to meet it, and was shaking the branches of a pine-tree to make the powdered tinselly snow fall off. Madame Stroehmann watched her daughter fondly. She could imagine what it felt like out there: the dry snow squeaking beneath one's boots, the sun already striking rays of warmth across the still air, that air so cold after the long mountain night that it froze the little hairs in one's nose with every inward breath for the next outward breath to thaw again. Or did children of six have hairs in their noses? She thought of Danièle's dainty nostrils, the little button-nose planted there deliciously between her big dark eyes. There would be no room for hairs, unless they were as delicate as those on a bee's legs.

Madame Stroehmann herself was not going out until much later, possibly towards mid-day. She had some reading to do. Every year, when Herr Stroehmann followed the wise custom of Swiss businessmen in sending their families to the Alps for the month of February while they remained at their desks in the city and came up to join the fun at weekends, Madame Stroehmann packed a big parcel of books in the boot of her Volkswagen (just a second car for shopping, but very useful and safe on mountain roads) and announced that she was going to catch up on her reading. She kept her eyes on the literary page of the *Tribune de Genève* all through the year, and bought books that promised to enlarge her mental horizons. No ordinary businessman's wife she. There was no economic reason for her to take a job and so she did not take a job, but she knew that the modern world belonged to the intelligent woman and she was not going to sit on a cushion and sew a fine seam while it all passed her by.

Danièle now came down the slope to the front of the house, immediately by the front door, and seriously set to work making a snowman. The snow was still a little powdery from its fourteen hours' freezing, but she worked seriously with her little shovel and her deft, well-gloved hands. Madame Stroehmann decided that the child would be safe for a while without supervision, and went to run herself a bath. She was still in a dressing-gown, but she excused this; it always took her rather a long time to bath and dress, and Danièle had been so eager to go out.

There was plenty of electricity, plenty of hot water, plenty of everything. Modern technology had brought instant luxury to these stern Alpine slopes; the old rugged mountain way of life was no more. Even among the few remaining peasant farmers, even among the poor people who lived in the shadow across the valley, there was probably no one now who had to keep an axe in the bedroom to break the ice on a pail of water before dashing it into his face to wake himself up in the bitter dawn. Madame Stroehmann lowered her elegant body into warm, scented water and lay looking contentedly at the clean wooden walls of the bathroom, the folded towels on their heated rail, the gleaming taps. This was how life was meant to be lived. She was twenty-seven, most of her time was still before her, and it would all be like this, clean and comfortable and spacious.

Outside, Danièle worked away contentedly. First she had to give her snowman a body: that conventional trunk, about the size of an English pillar-box, which is the base of every snowman's anatomy. The trouble was that the pillar-shape she aimed at would keep turning into a cone. Whenever she put a spadeful of snow on the top, it tended to run down the sides in hundreds of diamond-bright crystals so that the foot of the pillar inevitably grew broader than the head. It was a nuisance, but Danièle did not lose her patience. She was happy just to be shovelling away in the sun. And then the diamond-cascade, annoying from the point of view of construction, was so beautiful in itself. The rolling crystals of snow seemed to be rejoicing in the strong sunlight. It was like a joyous marriage between the element of water, caught and held by the cold in this new festive shape, and the element of pure light. It is not possible to behold such a sight without thinking that the creator is, after all, very generous and very merciful. Danièle did not formulate the thought to herself in those terms, but she felt it in her bones and her nerves and her blood-vessels, which is why she was happy.

She bent with her shovel and began determinedly to trim away the powdery snow that thickened and encumbered the base of her pillar. The busy swish of the shovel prevented her from hearing the squeak of boots on snow, and the direction of the sunlight at its shallow morning angle kept any shadow from falling within her field of vision; so that she did not know there was anyone approaching until she heard his voice, quite close to her:

'You need to roll a snowball.'

Danièle turned and saw a man looking down at her, with the sun full in his face, smiling. He wore a thick black overcoat of the kind more usually seen in cities than in the Alps, where most people wore zip-up jackets with fur collars. On his head was a green felt hat with a length of rope round it, Alpine fashion, in place of the usual band; the hat was old and looked as if some more prosperous person might have cast it off. But on his feet were good boots that looked new, and he was wearing the regulation ski-ing trousers caught at the instep.

He seemed friendly, so Danièle said, 'Why a snowball?'

'Well, two really,' the stranger said. 'A round one for

the head, and a cylindrical one for the body. Like that,'
he added, making the shape with his hands in the air,
since Danièle's face revealed that she did not know the
word 'cylindrical'.

Danièle was still unconvinced. Quickly, the stranger
stooped and with his ungloved hands fashioned a ball
from the loose snow beside the trodden path. Danièle
wondered how he could stand the freezing touch of the
snow, but he worked fast and skilfully, and the warmth
of his hands was just enough to soften the snow and
make it cohere. In a moment he had a ball the size of a
football; still stooping, he began to roll it forward,
collecting a feathery coat of snow. Straightening his
knees, bending from the waist, the agile stranger moved
up the slope away from the Stroehmanns' chalet, into
the dazzling snow-slope that lay now freshly bathed in
intense light. Behind him appeared a tripartite trail,
the long stripe made by the snowball and the splayed-
out imprint of his boots. As the child watched, he
moved ten, twenty, thirty yards; then, straightening up,
turned and smiled at her. In his careful hands he held a
broad cylinder of snow. This he carried across the path
and put it down on the verge at the other side. Stooping
again, rolling again, he came down towards her. The
snow log was thick and sturdy now, and as tall as she
was. The plot of land outside the Stroehmanns' chalet
was marked off from the outer world by a modest
fence, just three cream-painted slats, not high enough or
heavy enough to keep anyone out, merely a symbol to
mark the fact that at this point the world in general
ended and the Stroehmanns' property began. It had no
gate, merely a gap through which one walked, following
the path of packed-down snow.

By this gap the stranger halted; outside, he set up his
gleaming snow-pillar.

'Why don't you bring it in? Put it beside the one I was trying to make?' the child demanded.

'I'm waiting to be invited,' the stranger said. 'On this side of the fence, the snow belongs to just anybody. On the side you're standing on, it's yours.'

'Oh, come in and use it,' cried Danièle impatiently. 'I can see you're good at making snowmen and I'm just learning. You can teach me and that will be something to pass the time.'

'To pass the time?' he echoed. 'For you or for me?'

'For you, of course. I'm a child. Children don't have to pass the time. They just have lessons and then play. It's all just lessons and play, lessons and play. It's grownups who have to pass the time when they're on holiday. You're on holiday, aren't you?'

He looked at her, gravely but with a smile at the corners of his mouth. 'How d'you know that?'

She became impatient again. 'I think we're wasting time with all this talking. Of course you're on holiday because you're in the mountains and you're not working.'

'We're not wasting it, we're helping it to pass, and how d'you know I'm not working?'

'Because if you were working you'd be driving a snow-plough or building a chalet for someone or you'd be climbing up a telegraph pole with a loop of wire over your shoulder and a big belt to hold you from falling.'

'You're a clever little girl,' he said, 'but there's one thing you didn't think of. I could be a person whose work was to make snowmen. A professional snowman maker.'

'You can't be,' she said decidedly. 'People don't give people money for making snowmen.'

'I don't need money,' he said. 'The eagles on the mountain bring me all the food I need and at night I sleep in a cave with a big fire to keep me warm.'

'Who lights the fire?'

'It never goes out.'

'Why do you live in a cave?'

'Because I like animals better than people.'

'Are there lots of animals in your cave?' she asked.

'Some are in the cave. Others just come by to visit. The marmots bring me firewood in their mouths, and the chamois come by for a talk, and the kingfishers bring fish they get in the mountain pools, and the wild goats bring their wives when the wives have got too much milk, and they spare some for me and I squeeze it out into a clean white jug.'

She thought for a moment, then asked, 'Why do the animals do all this for you?'

'They like me,' he said gravely.

'Why?'

'Because I speak their language. I'm the only human person that does. That's another part of my work — I speak non-human languages.'

'I don't understand you. It doesn't matter. Let's make a snowman.'

'No, it's important. What don't you understand? Non-human languages? I just mean I can talk with beings that don't have our kind of language. I can talk to trees. But that's easy: I'm not quite the *only* person who can do that — there are just a few more. I know a girl who can. But there are some languages that I'm the only one to speak. For instance,' he looked at her impressively, holding her eyes, 'I can speak snowman language.'

'How can you? They don't say anything.'

'Not saying anything is all part of it. You have to stay absolutely silent and keep still and *think*. And there has to be snow all round. A snowman couldn't talk if he was in a refrigerated case in a museum. But if you keep quiet and stand still with snow all round you, and *wait*, then after a time words begin to form in the air and other snowmen can see them. And snow women too.'

'Are there snow women?'

'Yes, or else the snowmen would be very unhappy at night.'

'We have to make a round ball now, for his head,' she said, turning off all these strange new thoughts and reverting, as a good little Swiss, to the practical matter in hand. 'You'd better put him *here*,' and she cleared a flat space beside her amateurish cone of snow.

The newcomer followed her in, planted the snowman's body, and began to gather snow for the head. Once again he rolled the ball to and fro, but this time with a rotatory motion that formed it into a perfect sphere. Danièle stood by in mounting excitement, and when the head was the right size and he straightened up, she said with eager pleasure, 'Let me put it on. Then I'll have done something.'

Putting the head into her outstretched hands, he said reassuringly, 'Oh, there's lots you can do. You have to make his neck, for a start. Your head isn't just a ball standing on your shoulders, why should his be?'

Critically, measuring the effect, the child positioned the snow head on the snow shoulders and stood back.

'Yes, he does need a neck. I'll just pat a little loose snow round . . . like that.'

They looked at their work together.

'Like a man already, isn't he?'

'It's a beginning,' the stranger said. (But minute by minute, he was less of a stranger.) 'He needs arms. They're difficult: it's best to use a stick, but I don't see any about.' He glanced round the bare slope of snow. 'If we can't find a stick, I can mould his arms — he'd have to have them by his sides, as if his hands were in his pockets.'

'I think I could find a stick,' Danièle offered. 'In the firewood at the back of the house. I shan't be long.' She came back almost at once with three sticks. 'Choose one.'

He chose the longest and thinnest, then said, 'He needs gloves and a hat and scarf. Can you manage that? I mean, all that's your department. It's your house and you know where everything is. And what you're allowed to take.'

'I can find *everything* he needs,' she said, dancing off towards the door. 'My father's at business so he's not here. He has to see to a lot of business because he's important.' She stopped for a moment and looked back at him. 'Are you important?'

'In the snowman world, very.'

She nodded, opened the door and went quickly into the house.

Until she heard her daughter come in, doubtless to look for her and ask for something, Madame Stroehmann, as she lay back in the bath, had been thinking about her husband. She thought of him with affection: he suited her very well, made the kind of life for her that she enjoyed living. (Though it was a pity, the thought crossed her mind, that women seemed so often content to have their lives made for them. As you went to a dressmaker and had a dress made for you and then wore it, so you went to a man and had a life made for you and then lived it. Was that how things should be? For most women? Well, never mind them. It seemed all right for *her*. She soaped her feet gently, and put the thought calmly out of her mind.) She, Madame Stroehmann, liked being cherished; she liked it, on the whole, better than being thrilled and excited.

Herr Stroehmann had a round face and round glasses.

(In shape it was not unlike a snowman's head, but this thought did not occur to her.) One night Madame Stroehmann had had a dream in which her husband sat opposite her at a dinner-party. They were at a house she did not remember ever going to in her actual experience, but she was glad to be there; everything was elegant, and tall candles were burning. As he sat opposite her in the dream, she perceived that Herr Stroehmann's face had become an enormous nought, and that his eyes were two smaller noughts, and his mouth a third one. The nought-mouth spoke to her: 'I may be a nought,' it said, 'but a nought standing in the right place can turn a hundred francs into a thousand. It's noughts like me that provide all the good things of life, because we have the sense to line up on the right-hand side of the figures and not the left.' And she smiled at him affectionately and said, 'Yes, dear, do go on being a lovely left-hand nought.'

Madame Stroehmann ran more hot water into the bath, worked the soap into a fresh lather and looked down at her svelte but rounded shape. It seemed to her that it was desirable, though of course a woman could only conjecture what effect she had on men. Well, not quite conjecture; she could read it in their eyes. She *knew* she was desirable; her well-tended body was topped by a pretty enough face, and fair hair that she normally wore gathered back in two waves across her head to meet in a loose bun at the back, except for the front two or three inches, which fell in corresponding waves on either side of her face, framing it very prettily and also drawing the eye away from her only awkward feature, a rather too heavy jaw-line. It was a style that had been suggested to her by a very good *coiffeur* in Zurich at about the time of her marriage, and she had worn it ever since.

Desirable she was. Indeed, desired she evidently was, by Herr Stroehmann. He was an energetic man, rather short, thick-set, the type that naturally runs to a heavy musculature; she, who was slender and rather narrow-shouldered, enjoyed the feel of his thick, strong arms round her when they made love, and the broadness of his trunk pressed against her. He was running a little to fat these days, but she kept him to a sensible diet with foods like muesli and yoghurt — except, of course, for those wretched business lunches he was always having to eat, abounding in all the wrong things for him like cream and steak. But she urged him to select wisely from the menu and she believed he did. They were a solid, affectionate, trusting couple and their marriage was a good one.

Part of what Herr Stroehmann understood by a good marriage was predictability. He was energetic, he loved his wife, he had lusty desires, but when all was said and done the most important thing in life to him was his habits. Unless you had a basis of routine, you had no infrastructure from which to cope with the unexpected. Get to the office at a set time, devote ten minutes to thinking over the work done yesterday (Were the decisions right? Could you have improved on them after a night's rest?) and another ten to mapping out the work to be done today; then buzz for your secretary and open the morning's mail. All this at a time when the bulk of the work-force were just about arriving and getting into their overalls. Routine gave Herr Stroehmann confidence; it did not ossify him; it reassured him that the world was not melting around him into a series of unrecognisable shapes, and so he was able to be flexible, more so than most of his business colleagues. He would go far, was already going far.

Since his pleasures with Madame Stroehmann were so

important a part of the structure of Herr Stroehmann's habits, these tended to take place on Saturday night (because he did not go to the office on Sundays) or Wednesday night (because there was never much intensive action at the office on Thursday; it was a day for catching one's breath, and indeed some of his colleagues caught theirs on the golf course). For the first year or two after they were married, he had been apt to want to make love to her at any time when they happened to be in bed; after that, it had settled down, substantially, to Wednesday and Saturday. At first, when Madame Stroehmann became aware of this pattern, she had regretted it; but now she remembered quite clearly, as she meditatively soaped her arms, the point when this regret had died away. It was when Danièle was three and a half and starting nursery school. Routine had come to seem to her, then, a beautiful and supporting thing. At about the same time, she recalled, they had made the decision not to have any more babies (she had not enjoyed childbirth or nursing) and to let Danièle, who had plenty of friends among her age-group, be an only child.

Yes, routine, she thought. It was nearly time to get out of the bath, dress, and start her reading. After two hours with her books she would go down to the village, pick up a few groceries, and have an apéritif, sitting in the sun outside Les Lilas or Le Chamois. Good, comforting, solid habits, with no intrusion from outside. Then she heard the door open and Danièle hurry into the house.

'Mama,' she called.

'I'm in here, darling.'

Danièle opened the door and looked in, bright-eyed and slightly accusing.

'You tell me off if I stay in the bath for *hours*.'

'Come in, darling, or stay out. You're making a cold draught. And I've only just got into the bath,' Madame Stroehmann lied.

'Oh, well, you must have been dawdling, then, and that's something else you tell me not to do.'

Madame Stroehmann sat up in the bath. All of a sudden she felt naked in front of her daughter's penetrating gaze. She picked up a large bath-sponge and held it protectingly in front of her breasts. 'Darling, you can't have come in just to say things like that — rather silly and a little bit rude.'

Danièle shook her head importantly. 'No, I didn't. I came in to ask about Papa's old clothes.'

'Old clothes? Has he got any old clothes?'

'Well, some of his clothes must be old. Older than his new ones, I mean.'

'When Papa's clothes get *old*,' said Madame Stroehmann, 'he leaves them off and I give them away to poor people. I sent three jackets and a waterproof to the poor people who were in that earthquake in. . . .' She wrinkled her brow; where had the earthquake been? In what country were Herr Stroehmann's three jackets and one raincoat walking about this morning, giving aid and comfort?

'Well, I hope you haven't given away *all* Papa's clothes to poor people,' said Danièle, reproducing her mother's severity (they were very alike in face and manner), 'because I need some for a snowman.'

'A snowman, darling? How nice! I must come and see him when he's finished.'

'He's finished *now*,' Danièle said. 'All he needs is to get dressed. Like you,' she added impudently.

Madame Stroehmann leaned forward and pulled out the plug of the bath. Water began to drain out. She took a large towel and wrapped it round her body, and another smaller one round her hair. This gave her both the dignity of a Roman matron and a slightly clinical look, suggesting a nurse in a private rest-home. Thus accoutred and defended, she towered over her daughter.

'Go back and finish your snowman, darling, and I'll look some things out for you. Papa won't mind if we use his sports clothes, the ones we keep up here.'

'I need a hat and a scarf and gloves. Ski-mittens will be best. And I keep *telling* you, he's finished.'

'Well, you've worked very quickly, that's all I can say,' said Madame Stroehmann, beginning to dry herself.

'I had help,' said Danièle proudly.

'Oh? I didn't know any of your friends were about just now.'

'This one is.'

'Who is it?' Madame Stroehmann asked unconcernedly, reaching for the talcum powder. 'Jean-Pierre? André? Or one of the girls?'

'It isn't any of them. It's a new friend. He lives in a cave.'

'A little boy who lives in a cave?' Madame Stroehmann was amused. 'What kind of fairy-story has he been telling you? Who are his parents, new people?'

'He's not a little boy. He's big.'

Madame Stroehmann did not wish to be too protective with Danièle, but at this news she decided to come out and inspect the new friend. If Danièle considered him 'big' he must be twelve or thirteen, perhaps farther into his teens. She had heard stories of little girls being molested by adolescent boys, or learning sexual facts from them in quite unsuitable ways. And what was this 'cave' the boy had been romancing about? Some deserted cattle-shed he would presently suggest that he and Danièle should visit? Alarmed, she gathered her clothes and began putting them on: ski-trousers, sweater, fur-lined boots, a silk scarf at her throat, the same outfit as yesterday, no time to ponder.

'A hat, gloves, a scarf — shall I start looking?' Danièle asked.

'Yes, dear. The cupboard on the left by the bedroom door. There should be some gloves in the drawer at the bottom, and hats hanging on pegs. There's a scarf behind the back door you can have.'

By keeping Danièle busy while she herself pulled on and buttoned her clothes, she could ensure that the child had no more *tête-à-tête* with this adolescent boy until he had been looked over and questioned. Herr Stroehmann did not send his child up to the Alps to be corrupted by some pimply upper-school boy with uncontrolled sexual fantasies.

She supervised Danièle's choice of wardrobe for the snowman, rejecting one pair of ski-mittens because they were a favourite of her husband's (he would want to do a little ski-ing this weekend, when he came up for that much-needed break from work), digging out of the back of the closet an old woollen cap that she had never seen him wearing — acquired, perhaps, in a moment of caprice as a young student, and living its ghostly life till now in the shadow of clothes that were really being worn: bursting out now into garish life, the jaunty hat of a snowman on a February morning. And a gaily striped scarf. Because of course she was not going to be too solemn about this. The youth would have to be shooed off — or, at any rate, scrutinised very carefully and told not to take Danièle out of sight and earshot of home; but making a snowman was Danièle's fun, and it must not be spoilt.

Just before they went out into the sunlight she said to Danièle, 'Don't tell this boy about your ski-ing class, dear.'

'He's not a boy.'

'I suppose he's a man,' said Madame Stroehmann ironically. Of course a big raw-boned fourteen-year-old would seem like a man to Danièle, and she would be proud of having a man for playmate. *All too soon*, thought Madame Stroehmann, and she looked with momentary pity, a flash of loving tenderness, at her pretty girl-child. 'Anyway, don't tell him about the ski-ing classes. Just don't mention the matter.'

Danièle went every afternoon at three o'clock to a children's class held by Monsieur Narbel, the ski instructor. The other children were all from good steady families (all Swiss, no foreign riff-raff), and Monsieur Narbel was very patient and good with the children. So Madame Stroehmann felt perfectly secure in letting Danièle swish off alone to the nursery-slopes, about half a mile down the mountain, and come back alone an hour and a half later. It gave both of them a rest from each other and, besides, Danièle looked such a little cherub on her tiny skis. But this lad, whoever he was, must not know that she ski'd down the footpath alone and unsupervised at a stated time every day, or he might be hanging round.

They were ready, and Danièle was moving eagerly towards the front door. But before going out Madame Stroehmann obeyed a natural instinct and looked out of the window, to prepare herself for the encounter by sizing up her opponent. She saw the snowman with his round head and moulded arms, and she saw a man in a black coat looking at the snowman thoughtfully, but she saw no boy.

'Your friend's gone, darling,' she said.

'No, he hasn't. He wouldn't go, before we've got the—'

'Well, I can't see anyone,' said Madame Stroehmann,

swivelling her head. 'I can see the snowman, and I can see a man in a black overcoat who looks as if he's doing an errand for someone.'

'That's *him*, Mama.' And Danièle had opened the door and danced out, waving the garments, explaining about them to her friend.

Madame Stroehmann slowly followed. That her daughter's playfellow really was a man made things easier in one way, more difficult in another. No awkward adolescent, inarticulate but persistent, to be warded off; on the other hand, a man was an unknown quantity. Men, on occasion, did appalling things. They were a danger to little girls and also to grown women. Men, that is, who were in any way odd or peculiar. And surely this one, with his talk of — what was it? Living in a cave? — must be odd and peculiar. Well, she could telephone the *gendarme*. And there was no need to panic, at ten-thirty on a bright morning, before she had definite evidence that he was going to be a problem. Perhaps he was just a kindly eccentric who liked talking to children and telling them stories. Not a common type in Switzerland; but then he might be a visitor. One thing was clear; she must get out and investigate, show him that she was a presence and must be reckoned with.

She went out and the stranger turned to meet her. She noticed what the child had noticed, his costume; but she also noticed that while his ungloved hands were broad and strong from use, his face was not the face of a man who had spent his life in manual work. She also guessed at his age: about thirty-five.

'Good morning,' Madame Stroehmann said in a confronting manner.

'It is good,' the stranger agreed easily. He did not exactly smile but looked as if he might smile at any moment.

'Danièle tells me you have been helping her with her snowman.'

'It's not finished yet,' he said. 'Her special contribution is to dress him. That's a feminine gift anyway, don't you agree?'

She did not wish to be drawn into discussion, so merely said, 'She enjoys it.'

As if sensing that she did not wish to talk to him but only to question and survey him, the man turned to Danièle, who had now finished dressing the snowman and was standing back to admire the effect.

'Isn't he *real*?' she said.

The man nodded. 'Yes, he has the snowman's way of being real — that is to be partly like a person and partly like a snowman. But I can tell you one thing he still needs.'

'What?'

'Occupation,' the stranger said gravely. Moving the few steps to the house, he took hold of a broom that was leaning beside the front porch, and inserted it nonchalantly under the crook of the snowman's arm, so that the figure seemed to be standing at ease after working.

'There — he's been sweeping the snow from your path and now he's resting. Snowmen are very active: they have to be doing things, not just standing there.'

'But they can't move', said Danièle. 'They have to stand still.'

'Well, you know I told you how they talk, by thinking the words till they form in the air round their heads. Well, they act in the same way. They think about doing things and somehow the things seem to be done.'

'He's certainly a magnificent snowman,' said Madame Stroehmann. She had decided to be gracious; that, surely, would make it difficult for the man to be anything but co-operative. He would do what she wanted him to do, and what she wanted him to do was move along and leave her child alone. 'It was good of you to help her. She'd never have been able to make such a good one by herself.' She spoke as if the affair were firmly in the past.

'It wasn't kind,' the stranger said in a matter-of-fact way, not contradicting her, just giving her information. 'I did it for myself and Danièle just happened to be there and helped me.'

'Oh,' she said.

'I need to make a snowman every day. I'm a snow-man maker.'

'Oh.'

'Where I make them isn't important. Any patch of snow will do. It's the snow, you see, that offers the challenge.'

'The challenge?'

'Yes. With its whiteness and spotlessness. Like a clean white sheet of paper that dares you to write something on it. But it's more complicated than paper.'

'How is it complicated?'

They were talking to each other now. Danièle, who had begun by listening to their conversation, had become bored by it and begun making snowballs, ignoring them, back in her insulated child-world.

'One piece of paper is very like another,' said the stranger. As he spoke his eyes held Madame Stroeh-mann's. They were, she noticed, a light blue. Her own were what a passport would call 'hazel', changing with the light, and perhaps her mood, from gravy-brown through grey to almost green. 'According to how long it's lain, what the temperature has been, whether there was a wind at the time of its falling or whether it just fell straight down in big soft flakes that landed squarely

n top of each other. Every patch of snow is different.'
Ie laughed quietly. 'You'd know that if you'd ever
alked to an Eskimo.'

'Well, I haven't. I don't know any Eskimos.'

'I know many. I spent a long time in the Arctic.
'hat's why I have this funny accent. It's French-
:anadian.'

She had noticed, in fact, that although French was
bviously his native language he did not speak it with
he local lilt. She had been trying to place it, but he had
orestalled her.

'Are you an anthropologist?' she asked. Some of the
ooks she was so conscientiously reading were intended
o introduce her to anthropology.

'I've told you, I'm a snowman maker.'

He spoke so seriously that she felt annoyed: there
hould be limits to foolishness.

'Very well,' she said. 'It pleases you to be humorous,'
nd she half turned away from him.

'An Eskimo', he said, his voice calling her back, 'will
valk past miles of snow until he suddenly comes to a
atch that's the right quality for building an igloo. He
imply knows at a glance whether it's right or not. When
e finds the right snow, he gets out a special knife made
f bone — they have nothing made of metal unless
hey've been in contact with outsiders — and with
ncredible swiftness he cuts blocks of snow. The knife is
pecially shaped for it.'

'Why are you telling me this?'

'He never takes any measurements. His eye alone tells
im what size and shape to cut the blocks. Then he fits
hem together and they always form a perfect structure.
n igloo, his home. Don't you find that beautiful?'

'Why should I?' she said, looking directly now into
hose cornflower-blue eyes that held her own so steadily.

'All primitive peoples have skills. I'm reading a—'

'Please don't tell me what you are reading,' he broke in, not loudly but urgently. 'If you want to understand how an Eskimo builds his igloo, it is better to make a snowman than read a book. If you want to understand the skills of primitive peoples, it is better to put yourself in primitive situations than to read surveys and tables of statistics.'

Irritated, she turned away and went into the house. Immediately on shutting the door behind her, she realised that her irritation had made her do the exact opposite of what she had intended. She had gone indoors and left her child alone with the stranger, the very situation she had set out to avoid.

Madame Stroehmann at once opened the door and stepped out again, but the stranger had already departed. She could see his black overcoat, amid the glare of the white snow, moving rapidly down towards the village.

'When grown-ups start *talking*,' Danièle remarked to no one in particular, 'children stop having fun.'

But round the motionless head of the snowman the words formed in the air: *We begin today.*

That was the Tuesday. On the Wednesday, Madame Stroehmann gave Danièle her breakfast and sent her out to play, as before, but she herself stayed firmly indoors. She sat at the table in the front room, which was actually the kitchen, though it was large and comfortable enough to sit in; propped open before her was Malinowski's *Crime and Custom in Savage Society*, a book she had been told was indispensable though it was over twenty years old when she was born; it was, her informant said, an essential gateway to subsequent anthropology. She did not progress very fast with it because she was perpetually glancing out of the window to the patch of sunlight at the front of the house where Danièle was playing. Danièle was under instructions not to move from the area where Madame Stroehmann could see her, but she did not rebel against this restriction because she was making another snowman beside the first. When she was joined by the man in the black overcoat and the battered Alpine hat, Madame Stroehmann continued to read, merely glancing out of the window at more frequent intervals and losing the thread of Malinowski's argument. She kept wondering what Malinowski would have thought of the snowmen, supposing a society made up of them had ever existed. Would he have been able to develop some technique of questioning them? Perhaps he would merely have observed them, like a zoologist; after all, if they had no human language they would have to be studied like animals. Then the thought jumped into her mind: But they are not animals, they are people, snow people. Angry with herself for this foolishness, she brushed the thought away from the surface of her mind as one might brush snow from the shoulders of a coat. A sensible modern young woman — a sensible modern young *Swiss* woman, what was more — to be entertaining such sick, childish fancies! Not, perhaps, sick in a young child, in whose mind reality and fantasy could still usefully interact, but certainly sick in an adult with a fully developed rationality. Back to Malinowski! — after, of course, a preliminary look out of the window to make sure that Danièle and the stranger were working tranquilly side by side and that he was not taking her off anywhere or engaging her too earnestly and intimately in conversation. At mid-day she knocked on the window to attract Danièle's attention, and, taking care to put on a kindly smile to mitigate the brusqueness of the gesture, motioned her to come in. Danièle straightened up from her task (she was shaping the toe-caps of the snowman's boots) and talked for a moment to the stranger, then moved towards the house. As she did so, the stranger looked at Madame Stroehmann through the window and raised his hat in a courteous salute before walking rapidly away.

Was there something ironic about the gesture? She could not decide. On the surface, it was simply polite. Perhaps the politeness itself was ironic. But how, in that case, did one tell?

It does not matter, she said to herself sternly, shutting Malinowski with a decisive snap.

'Why didn't you come out?' Danièle demanded, entering the kitchen with her cheeks aglow. 'It's lovely in the sun. And we made another snowman for the first one to talk to.'

Sure enough, two snowmen confronted each other in confidential attitudes, one dressed, one naked.

'I didn't feel like coming out,' said Madame Stroehmann. She spoke firmly and rather distantly, as if to emphasise that it was not a little girl's business to question her mother. 'I was reading a very interesting book.' She realised as she spoke that she could not remember a single thought she had gathered from the book. 'Besides, we're going out now.'

'Down to the village, I suppose?' said Danièle resignedly; she did not enjoy sitting still while Madame Stroehmann sipped her apéritif.

'Down to the village.'

Outside Le Chamois they sat in the sun with glasses of appropriate liquids before them. Madame Stroehmann relaxed, nodded to an acquaintance or two, exchanged the odd 'Bonjour' and the odd query; normality came flooding back and she felt reassured. Life had not changed merely because a strange man, at a loose end, amused himself by making a snowman with a little girl, and telling her a few fanciful stories into the bargain.

'Did the man tell you any more of his nonsense?' she demanded suddenly, turning her gaze full on Danièle. 'About living in a cave and all the rest of it?'

'No,' the child said. 'We just worked.'

Her face was closed as it always was when she was telling an untruth. Madame Stroehmann felt a return of uneasiness. Was she being shut out of something? Ought she to be more vigilant? But what could she do, short of going out with Danièle and being herself drawn into conversation with the stranger? That was probably what he wanted. But then, who knew what he wanted?

At that moment the stranger walked past, crossing the road at an intersection about fifty yards away. Turning to look up the street, he saw Madame Stroehmann and, without breaking his rapid stride, raised his hat in that same courteous, slightly formal gesture. Mockery? Why should anyone mock her? What was mockworthy about her, Madame Stroehmann, expensively dressed, a young matron taking her sensible February holiday, sitting in the sun with her beautiful little daughter?

The question answered itself in the very asking. Or almost answered itself. Madame Stroehmann decided to dismiss the stranger from her mind. Nevertheless, that afternoon she walked down with Danièle to see her safe into the hands of Monsieur Narbel. She felt a curious reluctance to leave the child alone on the mountainside; as if it had, suddenly, become a place where the unknown lay in wait.

One of the older children, whose family chalet was farther on up the mountain and who passed the Stroehmanns' on her way home, promised to bring Danièle home. Madame Stroehmann walked back, alone and pensive, in the last level sunlight. Before her door she paused. The two snowmen — she could not fight down the absurd impression — seemed intent on their conversation, and once again she had the sense of being excluded. For a moment she had an almost uncontrollable impulse to snatch up a shovel and knock the pair of them to pieces; but she managed, just, to control it. Danièle would have been first heartbroken, then sullen; Herr Stroehmann, when he came up the mountain on Friday evening, would certainly hear the story; she would stand convicted of having behaved irrationally. She, a woman who had her domestic and marital life under control, who managed her household and gave dinner-parties, who read Malinowski!

Besides, what was so annoying about two harmless snow figures? She must get a grip on herself. Perhaps she missed her husband in unconscious ways. The silence and immensity of the Alps can do strange things to the human mind, as can the vacancy of the sea and the desert. For a moment, entering the house and throwing off her fur coat, she longed intensely for Friday evening.

On the Thursday Madame Stroehmann did not even sit downstairs in the kitchen. After sending Danièle out to resume her passionate snow-sculpture ('Aren't you beginning to get tired of making snowmen?' 'No,' said the child bluntly), she went upstairs to the bedroom she shared with Herr Stroehmann. When he was there, of course. When she was alone in it, she tended to fill it with her personality, hanging her clothes on the backs of chairs, letting her jars and tubes crowd the dressing-table. The bedroom faced in the same direction as the kitchen, and anyone standing at the bedroom window would have been visible from the front of the house, the snowman area (as she had now begun to think of it). Unwilling to be seen, Madame Stroehmann arranged a chair on the side of the room away from the window; the light was not very good and she did not want to switch on the lighting in the room, which would have given away that there was someone in there, so she turned her chair with its back to the window and resolutely opened *Crime and Custom in Savage Society.*

She felt strange, sitting there. The room was very silent. There was plenty of light, but since the sun had not yet reached the point of shining directly on the wall of the house, it was diffused light, seeming to flow upwards from the snow. The ceiling of the room was saturated in a subdued radiance, cloudy yet strong. Once or twice Madame Stroehmann wondered if she ought to put on her dark glasses. Which was absurd, because her eyes were in excellent condition and not unduly affected by strong light. But they felt disturbed. Every part of her felt disturbed. As for Malinowski, he might have lived and died without writing a word for all the effect he was having on Madame Stroehmann's intellect.

Had the stranger come? She strained her ears in the silence of the room. Was Danièle talking to somebody? Or was what she could hear only the faint desultory sound of the child humming to herself? Could she, in fact, hear anything?

Unable to bear it any longer, she stole to the window. Taking elaborate pains to avoid being seen (always supposing there was anybody interested in seeing her), she opened the window a few inches. Cold air entered the bedroom, but so did the sounds of the outside world. At the moment she eased the window open, a lorry was labouring up the road, all of two hundred yards away but distinctly audible in the room. In the silence that followed its passing, Danièle's voice said, 'Why a snow lady?'

The stranger's voice answered, 'Because there are two snowmen and they'll start getting lonely without a snow lady.'

'But they've got each other.'

'Men get lonely without ladies. Even if there are other men about.'

'D'you mean men? Or snowmen?'

'There's no difference when it comes to missing ladies.'

Madame Stroehmann moved away from the window and lay down on the bed, listening intently.

'I know men and ladies are different,' Danièle's voice came clearly through the morning air. 'That's why they like to be together. It's why they get married. Did you know that?'

'No,' his voice sounded gravely, 'I don't think I knew that.'

'They're not the same to look at, you know, men and ladies. They're a different shape.'

'Well, I can see that, of course.'

'No, but not just the bits you can see,' the child said confidingly. 'I mean when they take their clothes off they're different.'

'Really?'

'Yes. My mother told me.'

'Well,' he said, 'if your mother told you I'm sure it's true.'

Madame Stroehmann, lying rigidly on the bed, had a sudden strong impression that the stranger knew she was listening. That he had, perhaps, noticed that the window was slightly open; or even, with sharp hearing, been aware of the moment when it was stealthily slid into a gap. His voice seemed to be coming directly to her ears, as if he had his face turned towards the window and was speaking straight towards her. Or was it just her fancy? Was *everything* just her fancy?

'All the same, snowmen and snow women are different, as different as men and ladies, and it matters just as much to them. They can't really get along without each other.'

'Is it when they take their clothes off?' she asked in a matter-of-fact way.

'No, it doesn't matter whether they're dressed or not. Their shape is different, I'll show you that in a moment when we start to make one, but the real difference is all to do with the way they are *inside*. I mean in their minds.'

'How?'

Madame Stroehmann and her daughter, one unseen and the other seen, one calmly and one in turmoil, listened for the answer.

'They have different ways of melting,' the stranger said. 'When the sun shines on a snowman he starts melting from the outside. Soon, if the sun's hot enough, he gets all runny and begins to lose his shape. But he can melt quite a lot and still be hard at the centre. He can finish up as a hard pillar of snow with a soft coating. But a snow woman, she's altogether different. She melts from the inside.'

'How can she do that?'

'I don't know how. She just does. When the heat of the sun strikes her, she passes it all through to her centre. She turns to water inside while she's still cold, powdery snow on the outside.'

'Well,' said Danièle, 'why doesn't it all run out of her feet?'

'It does sometimes,' the stranger said. 'Sometimes she finishes up absolutely empty. Just this cold outside and nothing inside.'

'Like an eggshell when you've eaten the egg.'

'Just like that,' he said. 'And now let's work. These two snowmen must have a snow woman, or they'l start having bad thoughts and the bad thoughts wil make your house unsafe to live in.'

There was silence except for the scraping of shovels Madame Stroehmann stretched her elegant body out on the bed like a crusader's lady on a tomb. The sun finally reached the window and blazed in, making her feel as if she were caught in a gigantic searchlight, as if all the world were looking at her. Slowly, she got off the bed and picked up Malinowski from the floor.

That afternoon, when she got back from taking Danièle down to Monsieur Narbel's ski class, the stranger was standing just outside the garden fence, contemplating the two snowmen and the snow woman. The grouping of the third figure had entirely altered the ensemble the woman was between the two men, and instead of inclining towards each other they were each bending with loving attentiveness towards her. The three figures were touching, and that night the freezing air would surely weld them into one.

'Effective, isn't it?' he greeted her.

'Is that what you came back for?' she challenged him squarely. 'To admire your handiwork?'

He shook his head calmly. 'It isn't handiwork that matters. It's the human effect of it.'

'What human effect can snow figures have, except for the fun of making them?'

'They can help understanding.'

She moved past him towards the house. 'I haven't time. I'm afraid, to listen to your fancy theories.'

'Nothing that I say is theory. It's all praxis.'

Madame Stroehmann opened the door. At that instant the setting sun moved up the hillside and left the house. It was as if a light had been switched off. Suddenly the house was in dusk. She reached inside, without going in, and clicked on the strip lighting in the kitchen. Then she turned to face him, knowing that she would be a silhouette in an oblong of hard fluorescence.

'I don't know what your idea of praxis may be, but I heard you telling her a lot of fanciful nonsense about the difference between men and women.' To her annoyance there was a slight tremble in that voice she had meant to keep so firm.

'What I told her about women', he said, standing there amid the shadowy snow, 'was useful and will be a help to her. And you know it's true.'

'What's true?' she said, but her voice was scarcely audible.

'That they melt from the inside,' he said, and came into the house.

On the Friday Madame Stroehmann and Danièle awoke to find that snow had been falling earlier in the night and was still falling. The air had become much warmer and the big, sticky flakes were floating softly down through it, so close together that they seemed to be almost touching each other. It was impossible to see anything distinctly. Peering up the slope in the direction of the mountain-tops, one could not have said whether the snow-laden clouds had settled right down on to the higher ground, or whether the grey-white blur was simply the dense veil of silently falling snowflakes.

Danièle, kneeling up in the window-seat, tried to see what had happened to the snow lady and the two snow-men. Through the whirl of flakes she could see them still standing there, but the outlines were softened and all distinguishing features gone.

'You can't tell any more', she reported to her mother, 'which is the lady and which are the two men.'

Madame Stroehmann set two plates on the kitchen table and put a portion of black cherry jam on each one. The rich colour of the jam against the simple white of the plates gave her pleasure, like the veiled light and the unbreakable Alpine snow-silence that was gathered about their house and all the houses in the village.

'It doesn't matter, does it, dear?' she said. 'That one can't tell them apart, I mean.'

'Of course not,' said Danièle. 'When it's snowed a bit longer they'll be just one shape with three round knobs that were the heads. And they'll have a lovely time talking to each other. It'll be like pulling the duvet up over your head and talking to someone in the dark.'

'You've never done that.'

'No, but I bet I know just what it's like.'

Madame Stroehmann smiled and poured out Danièle's milky coffee. 'It won't be fit to go out this morning,' she said, 'so we'll stay indoors and do something you'd like to do. What shall it be? Read stories? Paint a picture? Play games?'

'I'd like to play games,' Danièle said. 'But not by myself. Only if you've got time to play with me.'

'Yes, I've got time. We'll do anything you want to do.'

Danièle champed a crust and said, staring out of the window, 'Papa'll be cross, won't he, that it's snowing?'

'It's not his favourite thing', Madame Stroehmann agreed, 'when he has to travel. But it'll be all right.'

'Why will it be all right?'

'Well,' said Madame Stroehmann, stirring her coffee and thinking, 'he'll have to come up on the train, and the train'll get through because it'll have a snow-plough in front of it. Then, when he gets to the station, if the snow's still coming down too thickly to drive the car, we'll walk down and meet him with the sledge. He'll put his case on the sledge and we'll help him to get it up here. It'll be dark and there'll be lots of soft snow and we shan't always be able to tell where the path is, but it won't matter if we fall over sometimes because we'll be dressed for it.'

'Papa won't.'

'Well, he'll have his big overcoat on, and his fur hat, and if he falls into a snowdrift we'll brush him off and give him a hot bath when we get him home . . . and everybody'll be laughing and making jokes, and we'll be glad it snowed and we couldn't take the car.'

Danièle clapped her hands. 'If Papa falls into a snowdrift you'll go into it too, to help him up, and you'll both roll about in the snow and when you get up you'll be just like a snowman and a snow lady — won't that be lovely fun?'

Madame Stroehmann answered her daughter's smile, and the child noticed that her mother's eyes, in the diffused light that filled the room, seemed less grey than usual and closer to a pure, lyrical green. 'Yes,' she said, 'yes, darling, it will.'

TERENCE WHEELER

The Philadelphia Connection

'SO HELP ME, next time that goddam schwarz has the noive to come in here, I'm gonna kick his black ass right back to the ghetto! I swear it on my mother's grave!'

'Your mother isn't dead,' I said from my desk.

'Don't rush me!'

Doctor Jerry Szerelmy, scholar, gentleman, misanthrope, clown and Professor of Applied Cynicism, slammed our office door behind his favourite student. The glass shook and the fan stopped again. His copy of *Rights of Man* fell over on its shelf.

Today he was very nervous indeed. His South Philadelphia accent rasped on every syllable.

'Can ya imagine the neck of that kid? Telling *me* what I don't know about George-goddam-Milton!'

He limped morosely back to his desk, all four feet eleven of him, and examined his breakfast hamburger for mustard. As well as students, he was also against mustard.

'*John* Milton,' I said.

'*John* Milton?' He feigned stupefaction. 'Ya mean he was right? Ye gods, they're getting smarter every damn year! Ya wanna bite?'

'Thank you, not at eight in the morning. Jerry, you'll ruin your stomach.'

'What stomach? Reginald, my years number fifty-seven, thoity-three of which were squandered at Aquinas Univoisity. I don't have any stomach. All I have in here is a space generously donated by my ulcers! Also the coffee's cold.' He poured it into the trashcan on top of his unopened mail and scanned the mixture as if for an omen. 'Ye gods!' he murmured.

I waited. At last it came:

'Well, are ya coming to the court with me or aincha?'

'You make it so tempting,' I said and deliberately took another student paper from the pile in front of me. It was heartless to tease him but to go anywhere in public with Jerry was to submit oneself to ordeal by embarrassment.

'Sarcasm I don't need. And from *you* I don't expect,' he reproached.

He waited for the effect.

'All right,' he announced at last, 'so don't come with me. Lemme face it alone. The story of my life!' He marched to the hat-stand and took down his new tweed jacket, bought for the occasion. 'Well, farewell, Reginald!'

'What?' I said absently. 'Oh yes, goodbye, Jerry, and good luck.'

He lingered, tiny in the doorway. 'Yeah. Well, goodbye then!'

'Goodbye, Jerry,' I said.

'And I thought ya were my friend.'

'I hope I still am, Jerry.'

'The hell you are, ya fink! Who took that Tennyson class for ya? Who lent ya his Gertrude Stein notes? Which, by the bye, have not as yet been returned to me.'

'You did, Jerry.'

'Right. And now ya choose to forget it in my time of advoisity. And I always believed the British were men of honour. Shit, there goes another of life's illusions!' He

posed against the door-frame. '"All's but naught;
patience is sottish, and impatience does become a dog
that's mad: then is it sin. . ."'

' ". . . to rush into the secret house of death, ere death
dare come to us?" All right, all right, I'm coming!'

'You're a white man, sir, a true gentleman,' he
triumphed.

'I'm a bloody fool.'

'That's what I said.'

'On one condition. You behave yourself.'

His gnome's face puckered and he spread his hands.
'Reginald, my child, what on oith can you mean? How
do ya like the coat?' He turned himself for inspection.

'It's very nice,' I said wearily.

'Yeah, that's what *I* think. Reginald, ya know, ya
have supoib taste.'

'Thank you, Jerry.'

'You're welcome.'

Outside, in the Faculty Office, his elation had already
evaporated. Father Joe Bruno looked up from his *New
York Times* and beamed:

'You're going now, Jerry? Good luck!'

'Thanks, Joe. How's the Swiss franc doing this lousy
stinking morning?'

'Going up, Jerry, going up.'

'Bully for the Swiss!' Jerry grated. He had sold all his
while the rest of the Faculty had stuck to theirs.

He walked to the entrance.

'Well, keep the Faith, Jerry!' Father Bruno called
joyously.

'Yeah, and you, Father.' He lowered his voice.
'Goddam Jesuits. Bismarck was right.'

'Lots of luck, Jerry! Ho, ho, ho!' Doherty, the
Faculty Chairman, noted authority on James Joyce and
second mortgages, boomed through his open door. His

Bostonian-Irish laugh rattled the windows.

'Thanks a million, ya hypocrite!'

'Don't be like that, Jerry,' Doherty boomed. 'Think positive. Ho, ho, ho!'

'Aah, shit!'

Their laughter followed us down the corridor.

We emerged on to the sunlit green campus and Jerry's spirits lifted. The students were coming from their seven-thirty classes. Jerry paused to linger on the steps where we often sat together in the sun between lectures, watching the girls. He, the father of eleven.

'Good morning, Professor!'

'Good morning, my dear,' he swelled delightedly. 'What a great day.'

'Isn't it though?'

'It coitainly is.' He turned to watch her legs.

'Jerry,' I urged, 'it's eight-ten. We have to get into Philadelphia.'

'I'm coming already,' he retorted irritably. 'Just don't push me, Reginald.'

'"No lingering! Force I must be brief."'

'And don't quote Gerard Manley Hopkins at me. Another goddam Jesuit fag!'

'I thought it appropriate,' I said innocently.

'Don't think, Reginald, *walk*!' He stumped ahead of me like a detained goblin.

We started across the students' parking lot, acres of newly laid black-top lined with everything from Cadillacs to Jaguars, hundred upon hundred. The temptation was too great and his pace slackened. Philosophy seized him. He stopped beside a cerise Pontiac Firebird, his head barely showing over its roof, and addressed heaven and me:

'How gross, Reginald my child, how unspeakably gross! Reginald, what times we live in. ' "The woild is too much with us; late and soon, getting and spending, we lay waste our powers. . . ."'

'Jerry!' I pleaded.

' ". . . Little we see in Nature that is ours. . . ." '

'Jerry!'

' ". . . We have given our hearts away, a sordid boon! . . ." '

I took him by the neck and steered him struggling across the teeming Turnpike to the High Speed station.

On the crowded platform he smoothed his ruffles. 'I just hope you enjoyed that display of brute force,' he accused me, conscious of his audience.

'I'm sorry. It was necessary.'

'Yeah?' He eyed me furiously, then softened. 'Well, you're forgiven this time. Anybody else, I woulda taken a poke at ya.'

'I apologise.'

'Right. Now then.' He surveyed the situation, the ranks of commuters opposite, the two sets of rails, and ascertained that this was indeed what it claimed to be. A rail-car passed in the other direction. He grew dreamy: 'Reginald, do ya know I haven't used public transport in twenty years. It's quite an adventure, isn't it?' He luxuriated in the thought for a moment then became vague and panicky. 'What the hell do we do now?'

'Didn't M'Lou tell you?' I asked, certain that his wife had not let him out without the most painstaking instructions.

'Oh, that's right.' He brought out a sheet of paper. He detested putting on his glasses in public. 'You read it. Her writing is appalling. A fine woman but virtually illiterate, it pains me to admit.' He cocked an eye at a blonde in a yellow T-shirt.

'"Take the 8:21 High Speed to arrive at Sixty-ninth Street Terminal at 8:32. Then the Subway to Fifteenth

Street," ' I read aloud. ' "In case you have forgotten, City Hall· is the tall grey building on your left with Benjamin Franklin on top." '

'Heh, heh, what a sense of fun she has. Any fool knows it's William Penn,' he chuckled grimly. 'I must have a word with her when I get home.' He turned to the yellow T-shirt. 'Good morning!' he offered gallantly.

She moved away.

'Suit yaself, kid,' he called, apparently unabashed. 'Reginald, doesn't it warm ya heart to see that womanly modesty is not yet vanished from the oith? A rhetorical question, merely.'

Nevertheless, his pride had been hurt. He looked about him for someone to pick on and chose a man of his own age on the other platform.

'Sheesh, it's hot, isn't it? Must be eighty-five at least' he called.

'I don't agree,' the man returned. Jerry had chosen well. 'It's more like seventy-eight.'

Jerry squared himself and stepped to the edge. 'What're ya talking about? Ya don't know what eight-five feels like?'

'Sure I know. This is seventy-eight.'

'Will ya listen to that?' Jerry appealed to both plat-forms. 'How can he say that?'

I had seen it all so often. I resigned myself and hoped that the rail-car would come quickly.

'I always carry a thermometer,' the man returned, bare-faced.

'Oh really?' Jerry sneered. He knew he had his audience now. 'All right, show us ya thermometer.'

'I don't have to show you anything,' the man parried.

Jerry turned to us. His face spoke his contempt. 'He doesn't have a thermometer.' He levelled an accus-ing arm. 'Ya don't have a thermometer, that's why!

Look, mister, will ya please do everybody a big favour? Will ya please don't be so damn childish? Ye gods! Some people!'

The man turned his back, vanquished.

'Heh, heh!' Jerry muttered, strutting back to my side. 'Sore loser.' He basked in his triumph for a minute then frowned. 'Where are we going?'

'To City Hall. You're in court this morning.'

His face clouded with recollection. 'Oh yeah, that's right. Oh, my God.'

'Jerry, have you taken your Valium?' I asked, looking 'Three.'

'It shows,' I whispered.

'It does?' he asked in wonderment. 'In what way, Reginald?'

I did not answer. I never did master the knack of knowing when Jerry was being serious, not with certainty. What difference would it have made? You played his game or did not.

A rail-car passed through without stopping, packed with students, clerks and blacks. The High Speed was poor man's transport largely.

'Reginald, do ya know how many blacks there are in this city? More than forty per cent. Doesn't it bother you?'

'No.' I was indifferent and that was the truth. I would not tamper with it even for him. It was not my city, it was not my country. I had bought my detachment too dearly to risk trifling with it.

'When it comes down to it, ya don't say much, do ya?' He looked at me with concern.

'Not if I can help it,' I said coolly.

'I worry for ya. Did ya know that?'

'You've no need to.'

'But I do.' He scanned my face. 'Mind you, far be it

from me to wish to pry.'

'Then don't.'

'O.K. But I still worry.' He switched his mood. 'Reginald, my child, all these people. We're breeding too fast, my boy.'

'You've made your contribution.'

'Don't imagine I didn't reflect on that many times,' he said grimly.

'Eleven times.'

'You're so right. Ain't that the truth!' Among his favourite roles was that of harassed paterfamilias. He loved it.

The maroon rail-car came in. We got on, dropped our thirty-five cents into the glass box beside the sour-looking driver, and pushed into the crush of black housemaids going home from their Main Line Philadelphia jobs.

'Ya see what I mean?' he murmured.

The car slid through the green woods and parklands of the Main Line. At each station, we packed tighter. I trembled. Experience of Jerry had given me good reason to. He seemed to regard life as one enormous storeroom of potential encounters, amicable or hostile as fate might decree, but always eagerly to be pursued. To him, a moment of isolation was a moment wasted. I felt him sizing up his neighbours.

He peered up at a big motherly black woman.

'Madam, I think this is your elbow I have here.'

'What's the matter with it?' she demanded from her height.

'Nothing at all, but I don't accept gifts from strange women,' he cracked.

'Well, I'm sorry about that,' she smiled. In her wisdom, she knew him at once as one of this world's comedians.

'That's poifectly all right,' he conceded graciously, unwrapping the remains of his hamburger and lifting it with difficulty to his mouth. He had his audience.

'Say, don't your wife feed ya?' she said.

'Indeed she does, madam, which is why I prefer this trash.'

'She don't cook so good?' she asked with compassion.

'She cooks good all right. She don't cook for me, that's all. Would ya believe, when I married her I was six feet one?'

'Dat de truth?'

'No, but it'll have to do for now.'

'She done ran off with some other guy?' She was a natural feed-man.

'No, but ya might care to suggest it to her. Say, do ya know my wife?'

'No sir!' Her chins shook.

He cocked an appraising eye up at her.

'In that case, aren't ya taking an undue interest in my private affairs?'

'Mistah,' she bawled amiably, 'I ain't touched your private affairs!'

'I should hope not!'

'Don't mean I won't though, if I gets de chance,' she threatened wickedly.

'Madam, that is the best offer I got all week.'

'Ya betta believe it, honey.'

'Ye gods, my lucky day! Who wants to go to City Hall anyway?'

'This is where I get off,' she simpered.

'Ah well, that's life,' he complained for the whole car to hear. 'So it goes.'

'See ya, honey.'

'Madam, I sincerely hope so.'

When she had gone, he confided to me: 'Say, what a

charming lady. But, er, did she seem a little, er, ya know, a little forward to you?'

'Not in the least,' I said, conscious of the eyes on us.

'Well,' he preened, 'I guess there's life in the old dog yet!'

The car passed from the lush Main Line into the ugliness of the city. It was years since I had permitted myself to express opinions about places. Nevertheless, one's responses remain. I thought Philadelphia hollow, harsh and mean. Calcutta might have mated with Brixton.

When we got off at 69th Street Terminal the driver, leaning on his brake, looked sourly at Jerry.

'Hey, buddy, are you on television?'

'Not yet.'

'Thank God. Will ya do me a favour? Next time, choose another car, will ya?'

We walked towards the Subway, Jerry's shoulders slumped and his feet dragging.

'But why did he have to say it, Reginald?'

'He has his troubles,' I comforted him. It was impossible not to feel for him.

'Yeah, I guess so. But what harm did I do him?'

'Don't take it so much to heart.'

'But I do, Reginald, I do. Maybe I should've stayed and talked to him. Ah shit, and for a while there I was really happy. What a shame, that poor guy. Ah, dearie me, the pity of it. That poor guy.'

His spirits sank deeper when we were on the Subway, and I, regretfully, was not the man to be able to lift them. He was such a child, his feelings so unmitigated.

'It affronts the eye and assaults the soul, Reginald, my child. Look at the trash. And the graffiti. Look at the seats all slashed. Everything all smashed. Ye gods,

what are we, men or beasts? What savagery it all speaks.'
His voice rose with his emotion. 'Can't ya sense the
anguish here, the hunger of the soul to rise, the human
spirit in bonds? Oh, the wasted years, the hours, the
very seconds, never to retoin. And they never do, my
boy, they never do. Private wealth and public squalor.
And the private wealth is pretty damn squalid as well.
Ah, the pity of it!'

The policeman sitting near us stirred uneasily.

The Subway came up into daylight and clattered
between walls of tenements. Jerry took it in for a while
in silence.

'And what of this? How did it all come about,
Reginald? Dear God, can ya imagine living out ya span
amidst this? What has American done to American, Man
done to Man? It ought not to be, my child, it ought
not to be! "Great God! I'd rather be a pagan suckled in
a creed outworn; so might I, standing on this pleasant
lea, have glimpses that would make me less forlorn!"'
he declaimed. 'We must tear it down, Reginald! Why
don't we, you and I, here and now? Why don't we?'

The cop got up and approached us. He creaked in his
harness and smelled of leather and gun-oil.

'Pardon me, gentlemen, do ya mind holding it down,
please?'

'Hold it down, officer? The time is *now*! Servitude
and the night of humankind has had its day!'

'Look, sir, it was a long night. I'm going off duty. I
get off at Twenty-second Street. Can ya save it a few
minutes?'

Jerry was touched. 'Why, coitainly, officer. Anything
to help.'

'Thanks, I appreciate it.'

'You're most welcome.'

'What a nice man,' Jerry was saying as we climbed the

steps and came out into the din of 15th Street. 'But do ya know what he had in his belt? Dum-dum ammunition. It can blow a hole through ya a foot wide. And such a nice guy. Why should a man have to carry death and mutilation around with him on such a beautiful day? And so polite. Ah, dear God in heaven!'

We crossed the street to City Hall. Jerry viewed it without enthusiasm.

'It was copied from the Louvre in Paris. Did ya know that?'

'Yes.'

'Pretty forbidding, isn't it?' His face darkened. 'The French filled theirs with beauty, ours is full of courts of law. The tower stands five hundred and forty-seven feet. It was gonna be six hundred, but this being Philadelphia some bastard had to skim the usual ten per cent into his pocket. So it goes. I guess we'd better go in?'

'How do you feel?'

'Frankly, Reginald, I would dearly like to go home to my nearest and dearest. However, no doubt I'll survive even this. Come along, I'll initiate ya into the American system of injustice.'

'You don't mean that.'

He girded himself. 'The hell I don't!' he grunted.

As we walked down the shadowy corridor towards Municipal Court Number Two, he said:

'Reginald, do ya mind if I ask a favour? Do ya mind if an old guy takes your arm? Beneath this rough exterior, I'm not so tough as I make out.'

'I had long suspected it.'

'I know it. It's why I asked ya to come with me.'

Judge O'Halloran was tall, crumpled and sad-eyed. He wore his gown over his shirt without a jacket, and I could see his braces. His collar was open and his tie loose. He was not announced and we did not see him come into the court.

'Where did he come from?' I whispered.

'He sleeps behind there. Look at the guy. His best friend is a bottle. Can't ya imagine how he got to be a judge? One day the Mayor says: We have to clean up the Municipal Courts. I need a man with the stature of a Lincoln. Somebody says: What about O'Halloran, he's six-four and skinny with it? I dunno, says the Mayor. I wanna a man who's kinda tatty so he looks honest. That's O'Halloran, they say, he ain't changed his shirt in years. O.K., says the Mayor, O'Halloran for judge. But if he moves, we're goona need somebody new in Garbage Disposal.'

'You're a dreadful liar, Jerry.'

'I am not. I had an uncle who was a judge. The finest man that money could buy. And it did, every time.'

'I still say you're a liar.'

'O.K., just let me babble,' he shrugged. 'So what do I know about it? I was only raised here.'

The clerk, a thin man in a worn black suit and as seedy as the judge, started calling the list of cases for the day. It was a long and desultory process because so few cases had their full complement of defendants, witnesses and lawyers present. The judge had to issue bench warrant after bench warrant, which he did with a weary and fatalistic patience.

'Ya see what I mean? Ya put the whole damn lot together, there isn't enough to make one decent trial. A travesty, it's a slaughter-house, a battlefield! Somebody doesn't want to be tried, they don't come. A lawyer can make more money in another court, he doesn't come. If I was the judge, I'd shoot the goddam lot and start again! Sheesh, he's got the patience of a saint.'

I looked about the courtroom high, grey and sunless; the families in conference with their lawyers; the line of sprawling policemen, some asleep; the judge with his elbows on his bench and his laconic pale face cupped in his hands. No doubt it was a room full of small tragedies. I wanted no part of it. I would allow myself to be diverted, even amused, but nothing more.

The first case concerned an elderly black who worked in a supermarket. There had been an argument with a truck driver about where some goods were to be stacked.

'He grabbed me here, your honour, here by the flesh of my back, right here, with his two hands, and he kinda threw me across the store.'

'He threw you?' the judge asked. He sized up the truck driver, a burly man, a typical redneck, seated unconcerned by his lawyer.

'Yes, sir.'

'What did he say?'

'He say: "Black boy, don't give me any trouble. I work for the Mayor."'

'He said that? He said he worked for the Mayor?'

'Yes, sir.'

The judge considered a while. 'Court is adjourned for fifteen minutes,' he said, and went out.

Jerry leaned over to me. 'Guess who's phoning the Mayor's office right now? Shit, don't try to tell me I don't know City Hall! Look at that poor old guy's face. Wouldn't it make ya weep?'

'No,' I said. The truth was the truth, I told myself. Why should I bend it just to cut a sympathetic figure in his eyes.

'Doesn't it distoib you that eighty per cent of the folk here are blacks? Do ya imagine it's a coincidence? Poor bastards, what chance do they have?'

'It doesn't concern me.'

'Reginald, my child, sometimes ya worry me. You honestly don't pity that old man?'

'Why should I?' I said.

When the judge came back, he postponed the trial for three weeks.

'O-o-h boy,' Jerry murmured knowlingly.

In the next case a policeman had stopped a car and found a pistol under the driver's seat. The driver was found guilty. The defending lawyer said:

'Your honour, the defence would like to thank the officer for the manner in which he gave his evidence. Thank you, your honour.'

'That's right,' the judge warmed. 'And he's a good cop too. How ya doing, Bert?'

'Pretty good, judge. How're you?'

'Pretty good. Have a good day, now!'

'And you, judge.'

I was amused. Jerry was outraged.

'Ya think that's funny? The judiciary and the executive hand in glove? It doesn't cause ya even a tremor?'

'It's not my country. Why should it?'

'If ya don't know, I can't tell ya,' he said disgustedly. 'And I thought *I* was the cynic!'

The third case began and Jerry was called into the judge's enclosure. The two accused youths sat by their counsel.

'Your honour, my clients were seated in the park in Germantown when they were approached by an acquaintance named Joe—'

'Joe who?' the judge interrupted.

'Your honour, my clients know him only as Joe.'

'Oh, *that* Joe,' the judge smiled.

'Your honour, he told them that his car battery was flat and requested their assistance, namely, that they should go to his father's car, a white Pontiac, two blocks down the street, and bring that battery to start his own car. . . .'

'Of course.'

'Your honour, anxious to help out a friend, they went to the Pontiac and were in course of removing the battery when a man claiming to be the owner confronted them and called the police. What we have here is a simple case of—'

'That's enough!' The judge put a weary hand to his forehead. 'Look, you guys, why do ya come in here with this baloney? Why waste my time? Ya know what you are. The Court knows what you are. You're car thieves. I know it. You know it. Two years' probation. Next case.' He shifted in his seat and stared out of the window with sad, intelligent eyes.

'Your honour,' the lawyer began.

'What is it, Mr DiLauro?' O'Halloran sighed, dragging back his attention.

'It has not been established that the damage amounted to two hundred dollars. The sentence is therefore inappropriate unless it can be so established.'

'I stand corrected. Is the owner of the car in court?'

'I am, your honour.' Jerry stood up.

'Mr Jeremy Szerelmy?' the judge asked with a glance at his papers.

'Professor Jeremy Szerelmy.' Jerry drew himself up.

'I beg your pardon, professor,' he smiled gently. 'Now what did they do to your car, professor?'

'Well, they forced the hood and one of the doors.'

'Uh-huh. In other words, they did a lot of damage.'

'Not so much, your honour.'

'Not so much?' the judge exclaimed. 'A new car? Let me put it this way. How much did it cost to fix? A thousand dollars?' he prompted.

I watched Jerry's eyes wander to the youths.

'Oh no, your honour!' he lied.

The judge studied him for a minute. 'So, how much?'

'Oh, maybe fifty dollars. I don't remember,' Jerry lied again.

'Let me get this straight. They jimmied the hood and broke open a door and it only cost fifty dollars. That isn't very much, professor. Ya must tell me the name of your garage. I'd like to use it myself. Fifty dollars?'

'That's right, your honour,' Jerry said stoutly.

'Very well. If you say so.' O'Halloran turned to the youths. 'It looks like it's your lucky day. It seems ya tried to steal the car of one of the few honest men I'll see here today. One year of probation and I don't want ya in here again.' He leaned forward towards Jerry. 'Thank you, professor. The court wishes you to know that it thinks you're a very nice man. Next case.'

Jerry came back to his seat and shrugged. 'What could I say? They were kids.'

'As a misanthropist, Jerry, you're a failure, ' I said fondly.

'Yeah, but ya have to hand it to me, I keep trying.' He glanced around the courtroom and shivered. 'Sheesh, I'm hungry. Let's get outta here, Reginald my child, enough is enough.'

In the street again, the traffic was deafening. It was humid and the sun baked the sidewalk.

'Why don't we go somewhere quiet?' he said. 'The Groves of Academe can get along without us for a while.'

We bought hard pretzels from a cart, his without mustard, and sauntered towards Society Hill.

'Ya think I'm a fool, doncha?'

'On the contrary,' I said with truth.

'Forgive me for prying, Reginald, but the four months of our acquaintance suggest to me that you are not a happy man. And that gives me pain, my child. Last year ya taught in Africa. Now you're here. Next year ya go to . . . where is it?'

'Brazil.'

'Right. Move, move, move. Why is that? What kind of a way is that to live?'

I hesitated, reluctant to put myself into his hands.

'If I went back to England, I'd go back to an empty house,' I said finally.

'Oh, now I see. I'm sorry. I shouldn't have asked.'

'I was married for seventeen years. I had a job that was bearable and a little more than bearable. Our own home. Two children. Then I met a woman.'

'Oh dear.'

'With her assistance, I contrived to persuade myself that life held more for me with her than with my wife.'

'My child, it's a very old story.'

'It took me two years to find out that I was wrong, by which time my wife was happy with another man and my children were sufficiently accustomed to another father. The other woman was intelligent, witty and as conceited as I had been. She also held it as her opinion that variety was the spice of life. There's a couplet by Rochester:

> "Womankind more Joy discovers
> Making Fools than keeping Lovers."

She'd had a businessman, and now an academic. She thought she'd try a surgeon. I was one of her fools, I suppose. No, that's not true. I knew what I was doing. As if there were not enough catastrophes in the natural way of things, without having to go and invent our own.'

'Ain't that the truth!'

'So I keep on the move. Novelty and work are great anaesthetics.'

'Things'll get better.'

How many times had I heard that?

'Ah yes,' I said bitterly, 'what someone once called "the cant of time". I don't set a lot of store by it. In my blacker moments, I've considered a measure somewhat more prompt.'

He studied me sadly.

'Oh boy, what am I supposed to say to that? Something like, er, suicide never cured anything? True, it does have a ring to it.'

We sat in the shade and watched the sunlight on the trees. The famous dogwoods were in flower. The cicadas' rustle moved in waves from tree to tree. The clumps of crimson azalea burned holes in the lawn.

'Ya know, I used to go to school near here. Saint Xavier's Elementary. Two things I remember. I remember the summer-time and how we used to go out on the grass with the nuns and make what they called the Human Rosary. It was beautiful, all the little kids under the trees, making the Human Rosary. What innocence. All the little kids under the trees, singing under the trees, and the sun making patterns on the grass. They don't do it anymore. I don't know why but they don't. That's a shame.'

His eyes filled with tears.

'And the other thing. When I was maybe eleven, twelve years old, I dearly wanted to be an athlete, a runner. Can ya imagine it? Me, four feet nothing and this hump? Ah, the dreams of youth. Well, I used to enter all the races at school and, naturally, I was always last. What else? One day the priest came over to me, another goddam Jesuit fag. He put his hand on my shoulder and he said: "Jerry, my boy, I'm gonna give ya some advice ya don't need. Always finish the course. Whatever you're doing, always finish the course. Ya never know your luck, all the other bastards might drop dead!" '

I helped him to his feet.

'Well, Reginald my child, leave us go see what the woild has to offer this lousy stinking afternoon. It won't be much, but I promise ya it'll be something.'